Joseph Ross

Songs of the Sand Hills

Joseph Ross

Songs of the Sand Hills

ISBN/EAN: 9783743369139

Manufactured in Europe, USA, Canada, Australia, Japa

Cover: Foto ©Andreas Hilbeck / pixelio.de

Manufactured and distributed by brebook publishing software
(www.brebook.com)

Joseph Ross

Songs of the Sand Hills

SONGS

OF THE

SAND HILLS.

BY WALKING HILLER.

SAN FRANCISCO:

A. L. Bancroft and Company, Printers.

1873.

PREFACE.

It was not originally intended, by the author of this little book, to give it publicity further than a few copies to distribute among his acquaintance; but, on consultation, concluded to print more copies, and commit them to the public. If, perchance, some of the within productions should engage the attention of the influential, so as to become in favor with the good people of San Francisco, then will the author feel convinced that he has not made a mistake in printing the within; and that his natural element in that direction is not a mistake, but is worth further cultivation, and he will endeavor to produce something more elaborate than this little experiment.

If it meets with favor at all, of course it will be in San Francisco, as most of the references are local, and pertain to San Francisco, of which the author is an old resident; who, if it had been his lot to have been cast in a more romantic part of this State, or among her hills and valleys, which is so inspiring for poetry, and where the wild birds' chorus wakes up the single note of the less favored birds of song. If such a part of the State of California had been his home, the result might have been an earlier application to the natural inspiration which has dictated this effort. But as an old sand-hill resident, being long engaged in helping the first run, or first spread of the wings, of civilization over our sand-hills, as a working man, and made subject to the summer winds and the sand-hills' bequests, together with all the many other anti-poetical insinuations, too numerous to mention; such as all old settlers have been subjected to in San Francisco, which is everything but that to inspire poetry, or inspire poetical ambition.

And consequently poetry, in the author, was as the notes of the bird, made long silent by the cheerless aspect of a long winter, until the spring time in life has well nigh stole away, before the effort to produce pro-rhymical verse was made by him. But the desire to put words together in rhyme, as is said in California, would once in a while crop out; until spare time was offered by the author becoming indisposed for a time, and which gave him an opportunity which suggested the chance to put together whatever poetical effusions are herein contained. The author will say, that, whatever style of versification he chanced to commence with, or adopt, such is observed strictly to the end of each particular production; and the rhyme being found more frequent than is general, as correct rhyming tends to lead the mind, he has endeavored that the measure and rhyme should be correct, and that the peculiar style of versification of each particular piece be harmoniously continued the same from beginning to the end of each piece. The wording will be found to be familiar and simple, and running smoothly, so that the mind will not get tripped, or thrown from the thread of narration, by either long or unfamiliar words or untoward irregular measure, after the mind is made up to follow a certain style of measure and verse; and, as these few natural rhymes were produced as a fountain stream which bursts forth in the desert, as an outlet or relief to a bounteous supply, so it is with the author, and if this little beginning is appreciated, there is an abundant supply from whence it came.

SONGS OF THE SAND HILLS.

SAN FRANCISCO, OR THE SAND-HILL CITY.

FOR a city to make far out West,
  Of the ocean's foundation and crest,
  In long years past away,
  'Neath the ocean's white spray,
  To throw up in a heap
  From the great vasty deep,
Rolling out, rolling in, then was planned,
To make mountains and valleys of sand.

Was laid up by the ocean to save,
Which she washed out from many a cave,
  In laborious toil,
  And sometimes in turmoil,
  To lay out a place
  Which time would not efface,
For a city to build of her own,
And which would be quite large when 'tis grown.

With what diligence ocean was blest,
And to never as much as want rest
  To accomplish her will;
  Keeping on to fulfill,
  And still cheerful with song,
  Through all time now so long;
Through each century's roll as they pass,
Making up all those sand-hills so vast.

And the wind must have lent her a hand,
For to carry away o'er the land,
   To fill up and to make,
   Both upon them did take
   For a city to build;
   For that purpose they filled,
For foundation to make and to lay,
Up the space between her and the bay.

With no limit of time to complete,
Nor with anything else to compete,
   Long and last they got through,
   And had no more to do
   But to level the drifts
   O'er the hills, which uplifts
Up so high, sending forth their bequest,
Left for mankind to do all the rest.

Now her mountains and hills looking bare,
And her channel, for nothing was there,
   On her bay, so remote,
   Nothing on there did float;
   On that channel so wide
   For all shipping to ride;
On that beautiful wide-spreading bay
Where the ships of all nations could lay,

But for man it was far from elate,
Isolated, and nought did invite
   Him that place to possess;
   But, yet, nevertheless,
   To this place they did come,
   From their kindred and home,
And in ship loads they entered the bay,
From their homes, which they left far away.

For the gold, which the placers did fill,
And which shin'd from the race of that mill.
   And in rivers was found,
   Soon was rumored all round,

From that place near beside
To the worlds so wide,
Causing men from all nations to appear,
From the distance so far and so near.

And to level the sand-hills they went,
And commenced was the building of tent;
  And in cabins to stay,
  While from homes far away,
  Was their buildings so rude
  For the miners so crude,
Made of lumber sent far from the East
Was their homes, while on beans they did feast.

Then the place for this city to be,
And made land from the wind and the sea;
  On its desert like frown
  Their had sprung up a town,
  And with plenty of gold
  Soon began for to mould
Into streets for that city to make,
Now was planned and laid out with some stake.

In her infancy now she was born,
Yet, in distance, and looking forlorn,
  Growing sportive and wild,
  Or the same as a child
  With the savage in wood
  It partakes of their moods;
Cut from civilization so far,
Or alone as the western star.

Then what wonder in strong ale or beer,
The report of a pistol would hear;
  As the world sent forth
  All her fast ones by birth
  In adventurous throng,
  There would some be among
Which no check or forbearance did awe,
For at first, there was nothing like law.

But what terror to all there was sprung,
In the tap of that bell when it rung;
  Started all to their feet,
  For the vigilants meet,
  And the citizens come
  To give trial to some,
And, perhaps, for beginning so fast,
Be hung from the window or mast.

Or, what wonder she grew up so bold;
For within she had plenty of gold
  At her will and command,
  As she now took a stand,
  Making business all round,
  With the world was bound
Unto commerce, and steamers did play,
As with shipping they entered her bay.

And the gamesters from Europe and France,
With their tables spread out to enhance,
  Or their piles for to make
  Said, come down with your stake,
  And your fortune to try,
  Then most all did comply;
For the gold on their tables did clank,
And as music it came from their bank.

How it makes one look back on that time,
In the days of that country and clime,
  When the simple invite,
  Which would seem so polite;
  " So come down, gentlemen,
  Make your game, gentlemen."
Count away on the table by run,
Then decide on who lost, and who won.

And those days of music and song,
With those tables surrounded in throngs,
  With the sound of the coin,
  Making notes to enjoin,

And the game made, perchance,
Might be won more than once,
For to build up credulity strong,
And to let all see nothing was wrong.

But what wonder, as already said,
To those vices this place should be wed,
While a stripling, so young,
From society flung,
Nearly out of the world
Was the male race here hurled;
Far away from their homes, where decoys
Took the place of the pure female voice.

But with all those devices and sport,
Which the youth is so prone to, in short
They are sure to outgrow,
And when better they know,
And when nearing the time
Of maturity's clime,
They will cut off those ways, and will plan
All the ways and the doings of man.

So the city which nature had said,
And so many which gold here had led,
From the world in quest,
Now began for to rest,
In reflection mature,
Now with motives more pure
Telling forth to the world in truth
She had seen all the faults of her youth.

As the blood in the races will tell,
So was found in her people as well;
As from everywhere here,
From all lands and all sphere
They commenced for to build,
And the city was filled
To the channel clear out in the bay,
From the sand-hills which stood in array.

Long at last she did get through her teen
Though chastened by the elements keen,
   Almost swept clear away,
   Both in June and in May,
   She was wiped nearly out
   Before water did spout
From her arteries and through her veins,
As sent down from those springs and those plains.

She has got to be full twenty-one,
But how many a pioneer's gone
   In her bosom to sleep?
   But how faithful did keep
   How they toiled to make known,
   Long before she was grown,
For to come on their track and make sure
Of the riches to all would inure.

Well, if now she is not what she should,
Imperfection is sure to make mood,
   She will all this outgrow,
   And the growth won't be slow;
   And when double her age,
   There are people engage
At a time when in years so mature,
In frivolities nothing can cure.

There are frailties which chronic become,
Always relished and cherished by some,
   Through all time of their life,
   And at all ages rife,
   'Till they sleep in their grave,
   Does their weakness enslave;
Though a century should be outgrown,
Yet their paths with the same still is strewn.

All must think now, and say she's but young,
If in haste she's condemned by the tongue;
   They may say in a haste,
   That her ways are unchaste,

Without thinking at all,
Where she came from when small;
How ungrateful to taunt her or jeer,
When raised up on a desert frontier.

But look not on her past, for its gone,
As she merged from the ocean alone,
    Without sister to give   .
    Her advice how to live,
    From the day she was born,
    Left alone and forlorn;
But when feeling important in place,
Then the world her saluted with grace.

Her proportions have merely matured
From the past lonesome life she endured.
    Now, the world's awake,
    Her acquaintance to make,
    And with bands reaching o'er,
    To her great ocean's shore;
For to join her in bands to elate,
In the distance which did isolate.

And to join with her sisters so far,
To enjoy what the distance did mar;
    As one family strong,
    For they alldo belong
    To the same stock and race,
    With the same human face,
And the same, by the eagle's great flight
To her ocean, before it did light.

Now she sits on her hills looking down,
On her head she can wear the bright crown,
    As a queen here she rest
    By her great ocean West;
    Of her crown never stripped,
    While her great bay eliped
For the world's great commerce to greet,
While they lay their bequest at her feet.

Reaching out to make commerce with all,
And the trade of all nations forestall.
  Nothing else can take place,
  Or can ere be the case;
  And the ground where she stand,
  Partly made up of sand,
Must outvalue all else on this globe,
When thus wrapped in her commercial robe.

As she sits by her channel so wide,
Where the ebbing and flowing of tide,
  Not too rapid to lay
  The whole length of her bay,
  And so sheltered and sure
  From the storms is secure;
With the ships of the world in her lap,
While outside her great ocean o'erlap.

And she sits at the side of her gate
For the world, both early and late,
  Giving entrance to all
  Sister States, great and small.
  This great country all o'er
  To the other great shore,
Where the wide Atlantic resort,
In her swaggering ways, as in sport.

To come back to our city again
In her splendor to rise all amain;
  In great beauty and power,
  Where her mountains now tower,
  As her pillars of strength,
  Passing through her whole length;
From her gate running off to the south,
And as shutting the ocean's wide mouth.

Who would not, as her child, like to be,
And look back on her greatness and see,
  On the day and the time
  When she gets to her prime;

When those places, now dots,
Join in hands with her lots
In surrounding her channels outlay,
The whole length of her wide-spreading bay.

With Goat Island, her center and heart,
Whose pulsations is felt to impart
   Through her lungs on each side
   Of its life-giving tide,
   Which all flows through her veins
   And arteries' mains;
All combined in one bodily frame,
As one city, one interest, one name.

She has made a grand start, and displays
In her young and her frolicksome ways,
   As her temples will say,
   In this time and this day,
   That her people, devout,
   For their churches come out;
Christianity, deep taken root,
In the sand-hills now under her foot.

While her domes and her steeples ascend
To the clouds ere they come to an end,
   Tells how fertile her land
   For their roots to expand;
   While their tops are in clouds,
   Or enameled in shrouds,
Sending forth from their steeples, which tells
In appeals, from their church-going bells.

And the synagogues' pillars, by day
And by night, which the history say
   Guarded Israel's tribe
   To the Red Sea; beside
   Emblematic is still
   Lifted high by the hill,
For his children to still keep in view
And for all generations out-through.

Many beautiful temples to view,
She has raised, and they must be all new
    To adorn her hills,
    While her people them fill;
    On two Sundays per week,
    Place of worship they seek;
One of Saturday, meets as of old,
By the prophets and patriots told.

And her schools, who can say she has not?
They are seen upon many a plot
    As the pride of the free,
    For to look to and be
    As the nursery seat
    Of this Union so great;
And the hope of the nation to hold,
As the youth of the nation they mould.

This is something of which she can say,
That her schools and school-houses this day
    Is so little behind,
    That it is hard to find,
    As her sister States tell,
    And they know it as well,
That her schools are an equal and far,
Although ages ahead of her star.

And her orphan asylums, how grand!
For a city so young, she has planned,
    Which some older States might
    Take some precepts, not light;
    For it first was her care,
    Soon as money could spare,
To provide for the orphans in need
Was accomplished with parental speed.

And no wonder she prospered so well;
For her poor, and her orphans as well,
    Did she first make a place
    They might have, and in peace

All their wants be supplied;
All was done while men tried
To make homes for their families too,
Having nearly enough for to do.

And her hills and her valleys now tell
Of these places she managed so well
　　To provide for the poor,
　　And her orphans in store;
　　That throughout her young days,
　　And her lone frontier ways,　•
Of those duties she never lost sight,
The neglected she never did slight.

And her temples of Masonry stands
That mysterious tie of all lands—
　　Emanating above
　　To make brotherly love,
　　So that men still can know
　　All are brethren below
On this globe, or this world of ours,
Which was framed from those temples and towers.

And her orders of different kinds
In harmonious ties which men binds,
　　All as brethren, indeed,
　　And to help when in need,
　　With a brotherly care,
　　And with such for to share
What was given to men to dispose,
Like true charity ne'er to disclose.

Oh, what beautiful things to behold,
And what blessings from them does unfold
　　To the needy and poor
　　As they open their door
　　To the fatherless child,
　　And their mother which smiled
On their infant-like days, but now gone,
And now left in this world alone.

But to tell all she now has within
Her vast borders, and who, and what kin,
   Would be futile to try,
   And must now pass it by,
   But accomplishing all
   When so young and so small;
Far away from the world arraigned,
And majority barely attained.

And the beauty and bloom, which foretells
In her youth, as her children and belles ·
   In her vigorous clime,
   In proportions sublime,
   As a land of the rose,
   Opening out to disclose
From its stem, in great favor to be,
And the world of wonder to see.

And her numerous banks and hotels
In her center, which always foretells,
   That the man of the day
   Here has found out his way,
   And American-like,
   With true aim, for to strike
For their fortune, far out in the West,
With that vigor, Americans blest.

San Francisco, now, but twenty-two
When she lives but one century through;
   When this short time, or near,
   On some morning, when clear,
   Oh ! how pleasant to look,
   From some corner, or nook,
For to see her in majesty stand,
Looking down on the ships from all lands.

But all must pass away as they came;
On their grave-stones there may be some name
   Of her old pioneer;
   May he read with a tear,

In her grave-yards inclosed,
·Where they lay decomposed,
For the time o'er their graves long has flown,
And the grass o'er their graves long has grown.

LINES

WRITTEN TO MRS. CALIF, IN BOSTON.

OH, dear auntie, how long
It does seem you are gone,
And to get reconciled are not able:
    If you knew how you're missed
    Taken out of the list
Of our circle surrounding the table.

You remember the day
We no longer could stay,
But in haste for to go to the wedding,
    How you stood in the door
    Of our entry once more,
And the tears from your eyes you were shedding.

How that same afternoon,
Came an hour too soon
By mistake in the time he'd to tarry;
    At that depot to stay,
    Which is called San José,
And while Maggie was cross as old Harry!

How "Scott" followed your track
The next morning in tack,
Round the hills as a chase o'er the mountains;
    Or across the vast plains,
    And the streams, or earth's veins,
Which flows on through her arteries' fountains.

I must tell you, of course,
Of the Square and its source—
Union Square is the one, I am thinking—
How the grass on it's grown,
Twice the same has been mown,
While the flag from the flag-staff is kinking.

Waves the flag from that pole,
Which stands now on a knoll,
And the trees growing up as been planted,
With the walks coursing round,
Or as Nature had found
Them, the same as been made, or been wanted.

The old National Guards,
With its tower in wards,
As a land-mark still stands as a station,
For that company true,
To the red, white and blue,
Or the pride of the city and nation.

And that church, built of wood,
On the Square, now looks good,
Though surrounded by so many shanties,
While it towers in height,
With its pinnacles light,
And is known as the church we call'd Aunty's.

Now, that this Trinity Church
You have left in the lurch,
With its arches of gothic so gorgee,
And that Sunday-school class,
You are far from, alas!
And no aunty has poor little Georgie!

We are all yet alive,
Still in three twenty-five,
But from you we have not had a letter;
And as Medas away
Now, the most of the day,
She's promoted, which makes her feel better.

And your room's vacant still,
For there's no one to fill,
Take your place, or the bed to look under,
There's the bed-clothes in layers,
Where you oft said your prayers,
And the prayer-book you often did ponder.

There's the stairs made so wide,
Where you still did confide,
That a trip you would make without touching;
With a man on each side,
O'er them you would glide,   [ditching.
When you're bound for the place where they're

Now I'll bid you good bye,
And I know you'll not cry,
But the cold's coming on which will splinter,
Binding up all that coast
With the snow and the frost,
Through the long lonesome nights of cold winter.

Then you'll wish yourself back,
O'er the snow-belt, or track,
Or before it gets covered by drifting;
If you stay there so long,
Those good people among,
But you'll say that I'm now only sifting.

How I'd like to be there
On that common or square;
On the garden where flowers are blooming
Through those long summer days,
Where the musical lays
With the sound of the cannon is booming.

I'll ask pardon from you,
And write something of Lou,
But it don't seem so long since they married;
For 'tis over four years
Since they left us in tears,
And away in a steamship was carried.

Before this, you have been,
And the darling you've seen,
Which her grandmother worships and blesses ;
If you please you again,
And embrace her amain,
And for all of us add many kisses.

And the rest of them tell,
That you left us all well
At the time you got off and was ready;
From the time you did pray,
Until that very day,
That the ground and the sand-hills were steady.

If they don't feel too grand
For to hear of the sand,
Or the shaking of this peninsula;
Never worse did it shake
Than that day your prayer make,
Since the natives drove on their first mulla.

WHIMS OF THE OCEAN.

WHAT is man or his time
    While he moves round in chime,
Or the sea, when 'tis raging in storm;
    When it rages so high,
    Coming near and nigh
To make little of all man can form.

What a toy does it look
On the ocean's great brook,
When away in the distance from shore,
    When it rises and falls
    With a hoarse voice which calls
To the winds in that sad solemn roar.

What the greatest of plan,
Which are placed there by man,
When the ocean conspires to possess,
And what means does employ,
And what cunning decoy,
As she rises to meet and caress.

How at times rests from rage,
When her anger assuage,
As reposing her children to see,
Turning over in sport,
As from schools they resort
To her surface so playful and free.

How she's quiet and still,
Drawing on with her will,
Through her veins, as in currents they run;
In such various ways,
Which so often betrays;
With her breath she eclipses the sun.

Then the beacon she dims
With her trifling and whims,
From the seaman and mariner brave;
How she hides all from view
From that captain and crew,
As he floats o'er her fathomless cave.

Then, at times, feeling tame
With monotonous same,
She commences to wrinkle with care;
And she puts on her cap,
Turns over to lap
With her tongue, as a lion in lair.

Then she moves to contrive,
And with cunning connive;
She makes motion more depth to display
To the world and all
Of her rises and fall,
Let them just think of her just as they may.

Then she gets in a rage,
Knows her time to engage,
In a violent passion to tell
To that vessel and crew,
What in rage she can do
When her bosom in anger does swell.

Then she dashes and wails
Till the heart of man quails
At her anger and maddening rave.
With what obstinate will,
She determines to fill
That brave bark with her mountainous wave.

But her fury still fails,
And but little prevails,
For the bark stands the storm so far;
Though she screeches and strains,
While the mariner fains
To get sight of the sun or star.

But her anger is deep,
She refuses to sleep,
And she rages still more in the dark,
And, while struggling, between
Her great billows is seen
The slim mast and the spars of that bark.

But outriding the storm,
The staunch vessel in form,
One sad, treacherous vein she employ,
While in raging and roar,
Draws that bark to her shore,
For to carry away and destroy.

When thus thrown on the beach,
Where the wild fowl does screech,
As by force, she still trying in vain,
Is in violence tossed,
And where all now is lost,
And one victory added again.

Then she reaches and draws,
When she man overawes,
To herself all the treasure in store
Of that craft, with the rest,
To her caves all bequest,
As a miser in hoarding up more.

As a miser indeed,
And as always in need,
Still a trying to get something more;
For as wealth still beget,
Those same ways her beset,
As a miser in laying up store.

Though her treasures so great
That no man can relate
All laid up in her caves down below;
While in riches she rolls,
From the lines to the poles,
And away where no man e'er can go.

Yet, mankind there is found,
With her treasures all round,
Where they lay in her caverns so cold;
Way deep down and remote,
While she o'er all does gloat,
They ne'er coveting all of her gold.

There they lay in death's dream,
'Neath the ocean's white cream,
In her forests of gothic and core;
In her depth do they sleep
'Neath the fathomless deep,
Where in pity she's covered them o'er.

Where no sound nor a tread
Is e'er heard near their bed,
As the ages and time pass away;
While her ebbing and flows
Still unceasingly go,
Till they're called from her depth the last day.

What account she must give
On that day when all live,
Or are called from her depths to come forth;
What sight must that be
For her dead all to see,
When she gives them all up at one birth.

With what sins and what charge,
By the wholesale at large,
She must answer for all of the waste,
And destruction and life
From all time in her strife,
By her rages of passion and haste.

GOOD-BYE TO '65.

THE year has gone, as all must go
Who labor and contrive;
With joys and woes it's past and gone,
Good-bye, old '65.

You've many seen put in their grave,
Yet many's left alive,
And many breathed first breath of life,
In year old '65.

You've seen great warriors yield to right,
With bands that did connive,
To part the bands of liberty,
In you, old '65.

You've seen the din of battle cease,
A lasting peace arrive,
The glorious Union all restored,
In you, old '65.

You've seen the dawning of the day,
  When liberty arrive,
And all the races here that's black
  Made free in '65.

But now you've left us to our fate
  As on this earth we hire,
And never more to come again—
  Good-bye, old 65.

~~~❦~~~

WRITTEN ON BECOMING A GRANDFATHER

NOW, how can this all be which I hear,
  As it falls on my listening ear,
    Coming sportive and mild;
Asking where is its grandpa and all,
And then asking the cherub to call
    On its grandpa, my child.

Is it possible this all can be,
That these accents directed to me,
    For to let baby know
How the name it will spread all around,
And I'm not reconciled to the sound
    Of a grandpa—that's so.

Still, the name is paternal, and makes
Me elated, and often betakes
    Of those venerable ways,
But now how can I think this is me,
With a grandchild here placed on my knee,
    In my palmiest days.

True an honor to be a grandpa,
But it strikes me with wonder and awe,
    For to think this can be;

2

It seems yesterday baby in arms
Was its mother, a babe with some charms,
  Sitting on this same knee.

When I take a look back on the time,
When all things of this life is sublime,
  But has passed now in truth,
Oh, how quickly the time has gone by
On the wing. and how quickly it fly,
  Taking with it our youth.

For it seems but a span since I loved
With the fervor of youth, which then moved
  O'er life's happiest ways,
And which chronic becomes when we pass
O'er that time on the dial or glass,
  Which marks noon to those days.

And which chronic becomes through all time,
When we pass through that happiest clime,
  Which we leave in the rear,
When no clouds came, or sunshine between,
Or the sunbeams of life for to screen,
  In those days to all dear.

How we cling to those days gone so fast
In our memory, as long as it lasts,
  And to youth how we cling,
And the same youthful ways to enhance,
If with fair ones we happen by chance,
  And those days back to bring.

And though faded the locks of our hair,
Still we love for to look on the fair,
  With that weakness possessed,
Which has chronic become, as been said,
From those days which are past and now fled,
  When we loved and caressed.

But although as a grandpa I'm placed,
They are chronic, and far from effaced;
   For I still love to be,
Where the form so divinely behest,
With those charming proportions possessed,
   Which I still love to see.

And forget that I am on the test,
With a grandchild to make me feel blest,
   With those thoughts so sublime,
But how can I those days pass so soon,
When it seems to me life is but noon,
   And the zenith of prime.

'Tis a pleasure, but must hesitate
For to think of, and now contemplate
   On life's short fickle stream,
That the name of a grandpa applied,
With a proof that cannot be denied,
   Or, can all be a dream ?

But from name I cannot stand aloof,
In the cradle or crib is the proof,
   While I see in those eyes,
And the same on the forehead and face,
All the parental features can trace
   In that babe where it lies.

But, when grandpa is called, I look round
For to see who is meant by that sound,
   Some one else it may be,
But in vain, for the look is transfixed
On myself, and cannot become mixed,
   But is all meant for me.

Then I glance at the babe which has done,
In its innocence, still as the one
   Which has started the fame,
While unconsious it sleeps there so still,
No account for to give for that ill,
   Of this venerable name.

Is it possible now all can say
He's a grandfather now every da
    And the name sounds u ncouth,
While I still feel so much like being young,
With a weakness which to me has clung
    From the days of my youth.

I can never, no never, get o'er,
Or the ways of my youth quite ignore,
    And wherever I go,
  Those of natural grace so sublime
I'll still cherish, though it be a crime,
    Whether grandpa or no.

LINES

WRITTEN ON BOARD THE " SACRAMENTO," ON A TRIP FROM
PANAMA.

GOD speed the "Sacramento,"
    Across the ocean's foam,
She bears the anxious onward
    To meet their friends at home;
Where anxious hearts are waiting
    And counting of the days,
By husbands, wives and children,
    Lit up by hopeful rays.

God speed the noble steamer,
    She bears us nobly on,
To our port of destiny,
    Towards the setting sun.
She minds her brave commander,
    On board no fear or strife;
Her ponderous iron muscles
    Stretched like a thing of life.

As on we pass, the mountains
  Are based upon the earth,
Their heads aloft are towering
  As wanting clearer breath,
While base, with thick miasma,
  Reposing clouds effaced;
There as a tower of Nature,
  But all a barren waste.

How Nature must have labored
  To give such mountains birth,
To look so grim through ages
  Down on their mother earth;
There standing in defiance
  Of ocean when it rage,
Or looking down in triumph
  Till getting bold with age.

Then listening to the ocean
  In silent awe so still,
Producing sounds so solemn,
  And air with music fill,
Which joins the world-wide anthem
  In songs all round her shore,
This world-wide surrounding
  With music ever more.

What singing and what sounding
  The ocean's shores make known,
Which fills the air with music,
  The great Creator's own.
The music must be purer,
  For all is pure within;
In oceans' solemn anthems
  There's no reproach for sin.

There's no remorse for evil,
  Those endless shores along,
No care or self reproaching
  Behind the ocean's song.

Continual she's singing
   To her Creator's praise,
For all His works of wonder
   He everywhere displays.

What harmonies of nature
   In that continual strain;
Of earth and sea in union
   All pouring forth amain;
All round the world's circuit
   Of earth's great sea with land,
For all the numerous wonders,
   The great Creator planned.

While forests' echoes sounding
   From river, falls and rills,
Comes sounding in the distance
   Was coursing round the hills;
At times so low and gentle,
   Throughout continual time,
And then arise enchanting,
   In sounds so pure divine.

While man joins in the music,
   With sounds to imitate
The glorious sounds of nature,
   As early heard and late;
With joyful songs and singing,
   With songs of Nature, too,
All join the joyful chorus
   With land and sea all through.

Yes, sing aloud with Nature,
   Ye winds the song convey,
Let all the earth be joyful,
   In one continual lay;
Pour forth the solemn chorus
   Throughout this world's sphere,
With all the songs of Nature,
   To him who plac'd us here.

LINES

WRITTEN TO MRS. HENSHELWOOD ON HER TARRY IN SAN JOSE
AFTER THE WEDDING OF MR. GEORGE SCOTT AND MISS
JOE HEART; AND AFTER THEY HAD LEFT SAN JOSE AND
HAD GONE TO SCOTLAND ON THEIR WEDDING TOUR.

NOW what keeps you away,
In the town San José,
From the prattle of Joe on comlummas?
And where all of the rest
Do join in the request,
In these long, lonesome nights from poor Thomas.

Now, as aunty is gone,
And poor Maggie's alone,
And for Ellen, she's cross as old Harry!
And as Medas away
Now the most of the day,
And now, why there, in San José tarry?

If you think of the past,
It was Saturday last,
It was Willie you told you were coming,
And then word came along,
Which made all faces long,
And the time which you set was sent humming.

Now the business is fair,
On the corner or square,
But uncertainties make us all frenzie,
For on Wendesday, they say—
Yes, they got it some way,
That to meet you went Misses McKenzie.

If you stay there so long,
In those gardens among,
And those trees, with their fruit nearly ripened,
Coming back to this town,
Where the sand-hills still frown—
With such contrast, you'll nearly get frightened.

Now the wedding is o'er,
And what is there more
For to keep you away, or what pleasure?
   For you saw them both start,
   And Joe part with her heart,
And how proudly George bore off his treasure.

   And by this they are far
   On the mountains, by car,
Where they traveled with Smith, the Professor,
   Bound for College McGee;
   They may all go to sea,
But the sea may become the transgressor.

   Now a letter has come
   For yourself, here at home,
And from George, which he wrote when ascending
   O'er the high altitude
   Of a Wyoming rude,
Where his time, in delight, he was spending.

   The Professor, at first,
   Did not care for to trust
To a taste for to make him feel better;
   But, when yet in the mood,
   He bethought it was good
For his lips for to keep something wetter.

   And by this they're away,
   O'er the ocean's white spray,
For the land of the rose and the thistle;
   From the steam cars, which shakes,
   For the old land of cakes;
From the sparks and the sound of the whistle.

   And approaching the rills,
   And the heath-covered hills,
And which Nature's own bard long have vented,
   Did a Scott take a start,
   And take with him a Heart,
To for better for worse be contented.

THE REIGN OF EMPEROR NORTON THE FIRST.

THERE'S no Empire or people can boast,
  Or can say, as they can on this coast,
    That they çannot complain
    Of their Emperor's reign,
But is blest with a peace, which his subjects display.
Arbitrary his rulings what no one can say.

There's no Empire so happy on earth,
As the Empire he has given birth,
    On the lands and domain
    O'er which he does reign,
In his island of sea, if had but embraced
Poor, old Ireland, which long has remained so
    misplaced.

Some will say that they, then would complain,
If our Emperor did them retain
    In his Empire of State;
    For they're disconsolate,
And a morbid dislike to all monarchs disclose,
His majestic sereneness would surely oppose.

He is happy now, just as he reigns,
And the spread of his Empire ne'er fains,
    Looking North now afar,
    To the land of the Czar;
And no jealous emotions to others does run—
Is the happiest Emperor under the sun.

A millenium reign he has had,
For no war was declared, which is sad;
    Nor the horrors of war
    Is ere heard from afar,
With those terrible charges for honor and fame,
Ere has tarnished or soiled his Imperial name.

Many monarchs would covet his place,
When the ways of their life they do trace;
    With remorse and with pain,
    For the number they've slain
Through their strife and their battles, and all of
    their deeds
Lurking still in their bosoms, the effect and the
    seeds.

While there is nothing of that to disturb
In his majesty's mind, or to curb;
    But as calm as a lake,
    He just reigns for the sake
Of being Emperor Norton, with Empire his own,
Over parts of Creation to himself is best known.

He has long been an Emperor here,
O'er this country and land of this sphere;
    San Francisco, 'tis true,
    He has seen her all through,
Her great trials in uniform, so all may know
That he's Emperor Norton, wherever he go.

And at home, in all circles of life,
And without either Empress or wife;
    And admitted by all
    At his beck and his call;
And is seen in the Halls Legislative at times,
And at others where reading and singing of hymns.

In a public or private display
No one thinks for to question or say,
    That his highness is there,
    With the young and the fair,
Looking on with sereneness, in Royalty born,
And is never indignant, or looking in scorn.

San Francisco has emblems she can.
And can count on as her's to a man,
    And the Emperor's one.

Never long time is gone,
Or away out of sight, for he soon would be missed,
For he's one of the oldest of sons on her list.

And now long may he reign to employ,
Those good tables of lunch he enjoy.
  O'er his city and ours,
  Where his happiest hours,
Where his first proclamation was issued at large,
To his subjects far off, which he still holds in charge.

There is one thing which still may be bad,
In his Empire, some trouble may add,
  If he passes away—
  He can't always here stay—
And an heir, that's apparent, there's none to be
    seen,
May embarrass his Empire, and trouble them keen.

But as trouble comes soon enough too,
And an heir may be had which will do,
  We will hope for the best,
  If he goes to his rest,
To an Empire more real and certain than now,
If, at all, is more certain, which all will allow.

WOMAN.

WITH Nature's impress how divine,
    With all now first in being;
Of all the harmonies sublime
    Which harmonize on seeing,
What is there of this earthly form
So much our planet does adorn,
        Or does refine,
        As woman kind?

She like the rosebud when it springs,
  So pure in human favor,
When opening in the sunlight brings
  To air its cented flavor;
Thine blooming as the full-blown rose,
With features traceable as those   .
      Of ancestors
      Come down in hers.

How conscious of retiring grace,
  So modestly and youthful,
Expression of angelic face
  So innocent and truthful,
Strikes man with reverence to know
That she for him was placed below:
      To love so well
      No tongue can tell.

What wonder then when angels seen,
  They are in female beauty,
While artists' aim have always been
  To make it still their duty
To trace her from divinity,
They all with one affinity
      Angels adorn
      In female form.

What wonder then the gods can see
  In angel forms so human,
Or that the star-lit spheres might be
  Adorned by angel woman.
For Paradise would still be lost
To all creation—man the most,
      If woman fair
      Was wanting there.

And what would be this rolling earth,
  With all its wondrous creatures,
So full of Nature's glowing mirth
  In all its wondrous features,

With ponderous hills and valleys green,
If there was nothing to be seen,
    Or notes so choice
    In woman's voice.

Her human heart where'r she goes,
    Ne'er waits she till to-morrow,
But moved in grief for human woes,
    With balm for human sorrows,
As round the couch with gentle tread,
Is bound to soothe the heart and head,
    As woman can
    For dying man.

This earth again would still be void
    As once when so alarming,
If mankind here were unalloyed
    With woman's grace so charming;
For light and life and all of birth,
Is brightened here by woman's worth;
    Earth to adorn
    Was woman born.

And home would be no home at all
    Without the lamp is burning,
Or in that home no infant call
    That papa is returning;
And she reclining on the gate,
With gentle chide for being late,
    And way is led
    To table spread.

With gentle tread and spirit meek,
    And pure the cheek and temple,
Still in her sphere will always seek
    To fill her place so gentle,
With home and children gentle words,
As mothers of both men and lords,
    In queenly pride
    There to preside.

THE SNOW AND THE MOUNTAIN STREAMS COMPARED TO THE LOWLY.

OH, the pure drifting snow,
　　See how pure it does blow,
O'er the forests and woods and the hill,
　　As it lodge on the branch
　　Of the oak tree so staunch,
With the home of the bird, Whip-poor-will.

　　Coming down from on high,
　　Coming nearer and nigh,
Through the winds in their hurricanes blast,
　　O'er that cottage and roof,
　　Where it stands all aloof,
Covered o'er from the snow on it cast.

　　How it tempers the air,
　　For the young and the fair,
By its winds, through the snow and the frost,
　　Giving vigor to all,
　　Through the trees, growing tall,
Till away in the tropics it's lost.

　　With its cold, frosty breeze,
　　Makes the rivers all freeze,
Their pure liquid is changed by the snow;
　　And the ice on the pond,
　　O'er its surface so fond,
Where they're gliding in joy, to and fro.

　　Made so pure and so white
　　By the frost of the night,
Lies the snow over all on the ground,
　　With that color so clear
　　As the corpse on the bier,
With a winding-sheet wrapped all around.

How it drifts from on high
As the winter comes nigh,
And makes light of the dark-colored ground;
What a contrast appear
When the snow, bright and clear,
Drifts away by itself in a mound.

How the icicles drop,
And the shutters do flop,
And the storm makes the forest trees bow,
And the earth covered o'er
Out of sight to restore
And give rest to the land and the plow.

Through the winter's long stay
Snow has all things its way,
And possession of lands broad and free,
Till the sun gets so bold,
Out no longer can hold,
Shrinks away in the streams to the sea.

What comparison be
More alike unto thee,
O, thou beautiful snow flakes around,
Than the beauteous and bright
Before knowing a blight,
Or a world before it has frowned?

O, the world's cold damp,
How it follows the tramp,
Or the snow, when it's pressed down below,
What a change does it make
On the pure fallen flake,
When trod down by the world as it go.

As the snow from its source,
Or its natural course,
To the beautiful springs up so fair,
As with snow on their cheek,
Or the rose-buds which seek
For to bloom while the snow-drops are there.

Once as pure as the snow,
Or a fount where it flow,
Was that creature, now seen on the street,
With her looks so downcast
For her sorrowful past,
Which her sex do all shun when they meet.

In the pool and the slum,
From the venom of rum,
On her cheeks, once as pure as the snow;
Once her father's delight,
With her eyes sparkling bright
In her head as she moves to and fro.

Yes, she once was so dear, .
That their life she did cheer;
If the joy and the mirth she possessed,
Or that natural joy,
Which themselves did employ
For to make her beloved and caressed.

With what love and what care
And devotion did share,
Through those days when so tender of years;
How her parents did watch
All her sayings to catch
In her joyful and child-like career.

And if aught ere but joy
Did their daughter annoy,
With what trouble and sorrow and fears
In a mother uprise
In foreboding surmise,
And would moisten her pillow in tears.

With what joy and what pride,
Or what had they beside,
For their daughter to them was their all,
And when winter appears,
Or their autumn of years,
As the trees on the coming of fall.

As they looked on the fair,
And on which the cold air
Could not pass or blow harshly upon,
As a rose budding forth,
Making graceful this earth,
Full of promise and hope to look on.

Now how can this all be,
On the street her we see,
As she passes along to descry,
O how altered she looks
From the corner and nooks
For to see who and whom she can spy.

Now can this be all so?
Has she fallen so low
From her parents, her home and all hope,
From her parents long gone,
To be left all alone
In this world with vileness to cope?

In the vilest of ways
She unfortunate strays,
In the ways of pollution, and then
In her scarlet she go,
So the world may know
She belongs to some infamous den.

On the street as she pass
She is shunned by the mass,
And the virtuous soon her descry,
As she passes along
In the midst of the throng,
For to see who or whom she can spy.

And her life's so impure
The unwary allure;
In her wantonous ways now is tossed,
By pollution and shame
Made disgrace to her name,
To the ways of all purity lost.

Can she now as the snow,
When so trod down below,
As it passes along from the throng
On its way to restore,
On that far distant shore,
Where it joins in the ocean's great song.

Yes, the source of the low,
When trod down as the snow,
All will find out the same as the sleet,
In that ocean's great main
Will be lost that dark stain
When trod down as the snow and the sleet.

And in joy join again
With that clear rolling main
In the glory and depths of the sea,
Going out at her ease,
Coming back when she please,
Now so pure, now so clear, now so free.

FORCE OF HABIT.

In California's early days,
As restless all with restless ways,
In numbers gathered here
To better their financial state,
And trusting fortune's fickle fate,
Had come from far and near,
But not to stay to make it late or long,
From homes and wives and children's playful song.

The spirit of unrest began
While tracing round our golden land
And packing round the hills
To prospect where the gold was found,
And searching for the place which crowned

The miner of all ills,
While echoes of some richer, startling news,
Of some rich strike which that unrest diffuse.

The efforts, after years so spent,
To settle down, needs no comment;
    To say at least it leaves
The self-same inclinations still
To travel here and there at will,
    Which very often grieves,
And very often is by habit's snares
Led on to evil practice unawares.

O, force of habits, how you dwell
In us poor mortals, tongue can't tell,
    Nor can it ere be told
How pregnant of those evil ways
Which we are prone to in those days
    When it gets fairly late,
And when the seeds of habits thus we sow
Impossible for us to them outgrow.

They take deep root in Nature's soil,
Then we may try and we may toil,
    Uproot them all in vain;
They still will sprout as doth the weed,
Which chokes the growth of better seed,   ,
    Which still we may retain,
From mother's care and early teachings left,
In us remain, from early days bereft.

From which that subtle root, Remorse,
Imbedded in us with such force,
    We never can uproot,
Which tells us to the bitter end
For ways of life to make amend,
    For vagaries we moot,
Which usefulness in life soon overawe,
The cords of which we on ourselves do draw.

Then Nature's parent will beseech,
Reversed to all his laws by breach
    Of covenant and will,
For pardon for those habits wrong
Which in us now have grown so long;
    His laws cannot fulfill;
But in our efforts we so often fail,
Our common supplications growing stale.

But all is good, for that was said
When man and all this world was made,
    With nothing to oppose.
This earthly globe can ne'er expand,
There's nothing less of sea or land
    That aught did e'er disclose,
Same world and weight, when at that time was said,
That all was good, that time the world was made.

There may be change on earth among,
By Nature's laws to source of wrong,
    Our mother earth possess,
But still it all belongs the same,
To that same earth and earthly frame
    No particle is less;
But still the same when Adam on it stood,
When it was made and all pronounced as good.

LINES

WRITTEN ON THE CELEBRATION OF A TIN WEDDING, AND READ
AT THE SURPRISE PARTY PRESENTING THE DONEES WITH
THEIR TINWARE.

WHEN earth and sea from nothing came
   So wonderfully grand!
The marvelous work was not complete
   Until the creature man
Was called to life as lord of all,
In paradise before the fall.

The great Creator of our earth
   Did see it was not best
For man, the first and noblest work,
   To live alone unblest;
Then while asleep, or did awake,
He from his side a rib did take.

And formed it into woman kind
   With symmetry divine,
With flesh and bone the same as man;
   So they may still incline
Towards each other while they live,
And hand in wedlock promise give.

With mutual admiration then,
   What wonder we still look
For mates, for we their offspring are,
   Came down life's stream or brook;
And make the vow divinely grand,
By Christian dispensation planned.

And marriages with bride and groom
   So often grace our hearth,
Comes down through all posterity
   To be of so much worth;
And ministers devoutly stand
To pledge each other heart and hand

This marriage then is called the first,
    And is considered good;
When early days are past and gone
    And wedding reached called wood,
Or "wooden wedding," as we say,
With wooden ware and wooden tray.

This wedding has been reached by those
    We celebrate to-night,
Is past and gone with years gone by
    In time and all its flight;
And as we meet to night as kin,
We meet to celebrate the tin.

Tin Wedding now; the time is reached,
    A metal not so base
For cooking puddings, cakes and pies
    So useful in its place;
A home is not the same within,
Without it's well supplied with tin.

And when the time for silver comes
    As tin has come to-night,
We'll friends and kindred be the same,
    And all things be all right,
And may the lapse of years unfold
The time in which to have your GOLD.

MISSION HILLS, SAN FRANCISCO.

BLOW on ye winds, and fogs roll o'er
  Your cloud-capped hills, which marks that
    shore;
  Those range of mountains seen,
They're soaring long and nothing marred,
And standing long as keeping guard
  For this Pacific queen.

You stand as sentinels of war,
When worn by time and care which mar
  The days of youth and prime;
Becoming old and worn and sear
Through time, while passing year by year
  Their period of time.

No green nor verdure there abounds,
No evergreen thy head surrounds,
  Nor aught but looking bare;
Though Nature others may have bound
With evergreens their heads around,
  She nothing you could spare.

Not even on thy care-worn face,
Scarce lines of vegetation trace,
  Yet firm you stand as placed,
With earnest same and sterling look;
By all creation long forsook,
  Is on thy visage traced.

You have so long deserted been,
And felt the situation keen,
  By human beings all,
Who sought more genial place and hills,
To dwell by winding paths and rills,
  And garden trees so tall.

While isolated and away,
Forsook by nature in array,
   You've stood yet firm and true,
And frowns of all was unaware,
Forgot, forsaken, standing there,
   Have nothing now to rue.   ·

With firmness you have stood the test,
Long washed by ocean's spray and crest,
   And that still solemn sound,
As Nature's works did thee detail
For that continual lonesome wail
   Which at thy shrine is found.

Nor had thy weatherbeaten brow
One tree to deck ere since or now,
   Or singing birds to cheer
Thy lonesome path; but that same sound,
One doleful note the ages round,
   Through time so far in rear.

How long in monumental stage
You've stood to check that ocean's rage
   Through time, no one can tell;
Or since you've raised your fearless dome,
And ocean told no further come,
   Although with rage did swell.

Deserted and long left alone,
For centuries there has been none
   To cheer thy lonesome night;
How dismal then has been the time
Through ages in thy lonesome clime,
   Through Time's continual flight.

Till long and last time did unfold
Thy sister mountain's virgin gold
   More favored than thyself,
By nature in their bosom hid,
And all their streams and brooks amid,
   And on their rocky shelf.

A gleam of hope then must have come
Across thy path long left alone,
   And looking on thy past,
And on thy valleys looking bare,
And on thy desert sand-hills' stare,
   A gleam of hope must cast.

Reflecting on thy dismal lot,
As here by all the world forgot,
   That yet the time may greet
That all this desert-like frontier,
May some day come from far and near
   And nestle at thy feet.

And from thy dreary spell to wake
To human voices and partake
   Of man's progressive way,
For long you've been in that same state,
No progress made, by change, by fate,
   But in sad lethargy.

But who can tell what fate may do,
When patience stands so firm and true,
   Or destiny have planned,
For to relieve a lonesome path,
Befogged or clouded long it hath,
   So long been placed to stand.

Now years hast past and time has gone,
And many a cottage, one by one,
   Has gathered round thy base,
And under thy protecting care,
From all the world and everywhere
   The human faces trace.

And from thy valleys echoes rise
Of progress and the whistle's cries;
   Of haste and speed which tells
That now you stand in union bands
With Eastern mountains, hills and lands,
   Where other oceans swell.

3

With cottages which dot all o'er,
Thy surface now is figured o'er,
    And domes and spires ascends,
To show thy barren hills and foot
Is fertile, for they've taken root,
    Which lasts when all shall end.

There nothing was while thus forsook,
For to inspire poetic look;
    Not as those mountains nigh,
Which did poetic song inspire,
Which Nature decked but to admire;
    Sierra's mountains high.

Where birds join in the coral song,
In woods and hills the glad year long,
    With songs in happy glee,
Which makes the world poetic feel,
Through cunning natures gently steal,
    In joy with all to be.

But standing bare, of verdure stripped,
As winter frosts her carpet nipped
    When putting forth her green
But for a day, then disappear,
Leaves that same color bold and sere,
    Is still for to be seen.

But as been said, you've stood the test,
And looking on your ocean west,
    While on its bosom ride
The shipping from all nations grand,
In passing in and out command
    With triumph and with pride.

And on thy bay so widely spread,
For commerce and to commerce wed
    Throughout this world around;
And view the works of man afloat
From mountain tops so once remote,
    Now to all nations bound.

O, Mission Hills! by ocean side,
By Nature placed there to preside
  O'er this great city's fate,
Thy destiny remotely cast,
Thy time has come at long, at last,
  In majesty of state.

How long those golden sunsets blue,
Has luster shed in golden hue
  Upon your western slope,
Which poet's bosoms still inspire,
And artists copy and admire,
  And still with Nature cope.

Thy Mission on a desert thrown,
Was long by mortal never known,
  But good when it can be.
For when thy hills, from bay to shore,
With homes and cots are covered o'er,
  Thy Mission all can see.

───✦───

THE WESTERN MAN'S TRAVELS TO CALIFORNIA IN EARLY TIMES, AND BACK TO SAN FRANCISCO

IN early days, near forty-nine,
  When gold was plenty, coarse and fine,
    On rivers and ravines,
When miners came from far and near,
And brought with them their food and cheer,
  Which chiefly was of beans;
For beans was made the early staff of life,
  With plate of tin and spoon, perhaps a knife.

There came across the plains which then,
And from his western home as when
  He left his frontier ways
To travel further west out here

For the far Western Hemisphere,
   All in those golden days;
He never saw a ship on sea afloat,
Or ocean wave which o'er the rocks does gloat.

Nor never saw a fish nor sail,
But that same plow and that same flail,
   Until he came to town;
At such a distance o'er the hills,
Across the plains and purling rills,
   While sunburnt dark and brown,
A youth he came from sunny south, or west,
From land of childhood which he loved the best.

His journey was not at an end
Till all is seen what time he spend
   In looking at the sights,
And ships and steamers as they play
O'er San Francisco's spreading bay,
   Which fill him with delights;
To see the motion of the steamer's wheels,
While wonder, admiration, o'er him steals.

Thinks how the motion of the steam
Is made to work on that great beam;
   And that great iron arm,
Clasped like a thing of life is stretched,
While up and down the crank is fetched,
   Like something on his farm
Which dreams through life, had oft annoyed in
   rest,
Or that great locust on his greens out west.

Before he goes back to the mines
To ocean beach he still inclines
   To hear the ocean's roar;
Went on the rocks where bask the seals,
Their wonder greater o'er him steals
   He never felt before,

For on the very ocean's caves and crest
He finds a—what is it?—a lion's nest.

They have no horns that he can see,
They have no limbs—what can they be ?
   How wonderfully planned,
And flopping up and down turn o'er;
Like lions as a lion roar,
   But have no feet to stand;
Some heavy as the body of a steer,
He now must think the critters rather queer.

Now in reflection turns away
From them; he cannot longer stay
   To hear them howl or bark,
But now the golden field must seek;
And filled with wonder looking meek,
   Is bound to make his mark,
With pick and shovel, on the river side,
   But hopes again to see that ocean wide.

And then find out what they can be,
Or if they live on land or sea.
   Perhaps there is within
That ocean great some bigger things,
In him with wonder to him clings
   And when he gets some tin,
The land and sea, and what there is or seen
He's bound to see, for now he's rather green.

He works away and finds some dust;
His pile is made, and now he must
   Write home to tell his friends
His luck is good, and soon will come
To see his friends and all at home
   Across the plains, which sends
A thrill of pleasure through his frame in veiw,
To think to meet his friends, his own dear Sue.

Yes, off across the plains again,
Where under trees has often lain,
  His farm again to reach;
At last is back from journey long,
Now all rejoicing, in the throng,
  Stands Sue at quite a breach,
For in his absence social song encored,
Has changed her heart, another she adored.

He settled down, some years thus spent,
And told all he had seen, and meant
  Some day to come again
To see the city far out west,
And mingle in among the rest
  Of mankind, not abstain
From knowing what there is in city life;
Perchance he might take back with him a wife.

For that young girl was now engaged,
Which made him feel so much enraged.
  When he was far away
A deacon's son had stole a march
On him, with shirt made white with starch,
  Therefore he cannot stay.
And now the golden shores again to pan,
Perhaps enjoy himself as others can.

He says, won't Sue feel bad to see
Me home with city wife; and she
  With jealous eyes will look,
To see her in the fashion dressed,
In glossy silks and satins pressed
  With Jonathan in hook;
To think of what a dash in fashion's lore,
With her I'll make in passing deacon's door.

He's rich enough, his farm and pile,
In west can live in honest style;
  Now back to see the bay,
And San Francisco large has grown

Since he has seen it, he must own—
   With wonder, now must say—
To see the spires and towers ascend so high,
Makes him look back on frontier life and sigh.

He thinks then to himself and say,
If I am here to stop or stay
   I want a beaver hat;
A beaver hat, with suit of brown,
So when I'm passing through this town,
   Not hear the word, who's that ?
While passing through the throng I often hear,
And beauty shying off as I come near.

Now to the tailor goes to get,
To see if anything will set
   On him, or find a fit;
When everything he tries is small
Or short, for he is large and tall,
   But still the tailor's wit:
Or bearded man, with hair and color black,
Persuaded him they were a fit and whack.

He's in the suit of black or blue,
The first one which ere to him clew.
   He feels them very tight,
And hugs him close about the arm,
And cannot stoop for fear of harm,
   Though tries with all his might.
And tries to seat himself upon a chair,
But finds they grasp him round and everywhere.

Now wants to shape some plan or way
To get acquainted while he stay,
   For now he wants a wife
Away with him to live on farm.
Some city maiden might him charm,
   And live with him for life;
And for this purpose, sought some one to know
Who could him tell, what ladies want a beaux ?

No one he wanted who had been,
Or over twenty-five had seen—
　　For widows did not care—
And some one not so tall as he.
She might good looking likewise be,
　　His joys and sorrows share;
And one who would not hesitate to go
To live with him in places high or low.

A friend he made, with whom he went
To visit those on marriage bent,
　　For George could well him tell.
He asked what lady sits beside
The one with bonnet as a bride?
　　George say: That's Mrs. Bell.
She has been married once before—bereft;
Her present husband's gone away and left.

The place they were was at a ball,
And we will call it Howard Hall,
　　Where beauty did appear.
While Jonathan and George did sit
To see the fashions—see them flit
　　In fashion's front and rear.
While Jonathan those questions George did ask;
While George did answer him when put to task.

He asks again, What girl is that
Now leaning o'er with a white hat?
　　George says: That's Mrs. Morse.
She has not got entirely free;
Her papers has not got to be,
　　Or clear with her divorce.
But when she does, she'll make a splendid wife;
She's never married been but twice in life.

Well, what young girl is that, whose hair
Is o'er her shoulders very fair,
　　And looking now this way?
O, that is Misses Mary Young.

Her husband has an awful tongue,
  She could not with him stay;
She'll soon be through the mill and free again;
Her second husband's on the raging main.

Then what young fair now on the seat,
She looks so young, with nimble feet?
  O, that is Mrs. Smith.
Her husband went away one day;
He was her third one, some do say:
  He did not have much myth.
But whether she has been divorced or not
I cannot tell; he was a drunken sot.   •

I'll ask once more what fine young maid,
Who seems so timid and afraid
  To meet a stranger, tell
She cannot ever married be?
She's but a child and must be free;
  She seems to be a belle.
I cannot tell the name now certain true,
I think the name of her last husband's Shue.

There is but one I'll ask you more,
The one whose hat is on before,
  That shies when I come near,
And looks at you with sparkling glance
With those black eyes, as though from France?
  O, that is Mrs. Clear:
She's been engaged, but broken off some time;
Her husband now imprisoned is for crime.

He says again now to his friend,
His countryman, his ear to lend,
  Inquire he must again.
What noble looking woman's that
Who on the seat beside you sat?
  Her name is Mrs. Fain;
She's not divorced yet from her husband quite,
Her fifth one now is watching her for spite.

Well, who is that, her cheeks so red,
Who spoke to you and turned and fled,
   With frightened looks at me?
Well I will tell you all the truth;
Her name at present's Mrs. Couth.
   No more you will her see;
The husband which she married last is round,
The other, too, is here divorced and sound.

We met a girl by the street,
Her hair was spread one solid sheet;
   She looked at me and laughed.
Now if you tell me who she is—
Her hair is dark, one solid phiz?
   I turned around and coughed.
Well, that is little Mrs. Short I know;
Her second husband's not divorced—no go.

My ebenezer here I'll raise,
And I'll be darned if that don't saize
   On me, and now to know
If all your San Francisco fair
Is all divorced and then did stare,
   Why how the world does go!
If that's the way the world has gone of late,
I am away behind its time and state.

For in my frontier days a wife,
When that was made so during life,
   To get the second man
They looked upon it bad enough;
Indeed they thought it rather rough,
   For woman, when she can,
To ever marry when first husband's dead,
It's thought the first one haunts the second's bed.

That's all old women's talk and stuff,
George looking now a little gruff
   To find him as a child;
Why you will never married be;

If you but listen unto me,
    A wife you'll get that's mild.
Why all the marriages are widows near,
Either divorced or husband's gone out here.

I'll ne'er get married in the mines,
What I was taught I still incline.
    I'll try once more your help:
There is a lady lady-like,
My mind and fancy much does strike,
    If some one does not yelp.
If you will introduce me to her once,
I'll try and work my way and take my chance.

With all my heart, who can she be ?
I'll take you with me and her see
    This evening and her meet.
Her hair is yellow, blonde and red;
She surely never has been wed:
    I tell you she looks sweet.
This evening you may come and her you'll see,
So you may see she looks both bland and free.

They went together and did meet
The fair one on the very street.
    And George her slightly knew,
Enough to open up the stream
Of love which followed then by ream,
    With vows for to be true;
And married be as soon as e'er they could;
He owned a farm on which to live they should.

One night he saw her home, and sat
Beside her by the rug or mat,
    When she got up to see;
And said, I must my curls take
From off my head, just for your sake
    Beside you I can be.
She then appeared so altered; hair was gone.
The very head itself seemed not the one.

What hair there was left on was gray,
And scattered o'er as in array
 To cover up the bare.
Then she sat down by his new clothes,
Upon the sofa as a rose,
 But faded I declare.
Near passed away before it is possessed,
Or e'en before by human hand been pressed.

He takes a look as on the sly,
Or from his seat, now looking shy,
 And thinks, can that be she ?
And stammers out, the night is warm,
Confound the flies, now, how they swarm.
 He thinks, if e'er I see
Such change in short acquaintance as appear.
She drew her chair some closer to him and near.

The chalk, a powder on her face,
Had worn off; left one red place.
 A pimpled face and cheek,
With eyebrows of a grayish cast,
Came peering through the black at last.
 Bnt still she looked so meek,
And quite composed and happy with her choice,
The distance closed on Jonathan, no noise.

He changed, his foot was underneath,
And turning, looking at her teeth
 The upper ones had fell,
And left a dark and ghastly breach
Between her upper gums and each.
 He looks and says, O, well!
Or what can that be, on such hinges hung?
 Thinks piece by piece she comes apart, as strung.

Of dentistry he ne'er had known,
His teeth were now as when they're grown,
 As all the folks at home.
Perhaps, a tooth-ache now and then,

Was all that troubled since or when,
  As dentists ere had come
Within so many miles of where he spent
His early days, or in that town or tent.

And all was new to him he saw,
Her teeth had left her gum or jaw,
  Then what was to come next?
Again she says, the night is warm!
If I should part with little charm?
  He then became perplexed.
If I should change my dress you will not mind?
To now get up and leave, he's is inclined

Consenting, she now on her feet,
With figure now perfection sweet,
  With toilet now so fair.
Returning changed, so much in grace,
His visage now with a long face,
  Unconscious says, Who's there?
'Tis me, my dear. It was so close and warm,
I knew to change a little was no harm.

She stands now up as straight's a pole,
Right up and down, which o'er him stole
  Reflections of this kind:
What must the women here be made?
What changes come, and how they fade;
  Now what is left behind?
To make a wife of when of Art so stripped,
I'll try no more, and from the house he slipped.

Next morning, when he did awake,
Reflections of this kind did make :
  They either are divorced
Or made of artificial gear;
I'll try no more away out here.
  And then away he coursed
To dwell with people after all whose made
By Nature's hand, through rural life and shade.

Now time had passed away again,
The deacon's son, he had been slain
    By Indian tribes, who came
In raids on frontier life to prey,
His rival now had passed away,
    And now he was at home.
Coquettish ways again the flame inspired,
He married Sue, the one he first admired.

LINES

WRITTEN TO MISS MARY M'QUEEN.

[On year of dry Summer in New England, 1864. Rain commenced while writing.]

HOW Nature sometimes will mistake,
    As well as we poor mortals;
That time that Nature needs the most,
    The time she shuts her portals.
        But still it's very true,
        I know, and so do you,
In early Spring the rain came down,
And Nature's efforts seemed to crown.

And blossoms from the fruit trees came,
    And flowers burst forth in splendor,
And everything gave promise that
    We'd have a rich November;
        But Mary, you know well,
        As well as tongue can tell,
Since Nature sorrowed so severe,
That she refused to shed one tear.

The consequence we soon beheld,
    For all things seemed dejected,
And like a maid that's growing old,
    Or some one that's rejected,

And hankering, hankering, fed
The worms both black and red,
Till all of Nature lost her prime,
And devastation reigned sublime.

In fact the face of all the earth
Was losing of her beard,
But though she's reckoned very old,
In Spring its still restored,
With ocean large and salt,
With that I'll not find fault,
But I would really like to see
Why people know its he or she.

But as the earth, whate'er it be,
Was blushing red with shame
That all her veins were drying up
Throughout her withered frame.
Her caverns of health,
With all her massive wealth,
Could not refreshing dews restore,
From sea distilled upon the shore.

Nor would the prayer divinely said
By ministers devout,
Though from the rock old Moses' rod
Caused streams refreshing spout,
Nor Lisa's prayer prevail,
Nor Albert with his pail,
Though water carried, long to tell,
In buckets from the deepest well.

But, hark! what is it now I hear,
Now patting the dry earth?
Can that be what was wished for long,
To all things so much worth?
Yes, croaking toads, give up,
Refreshing globules sup,
And call all nature praise to rise,
The earth is nourished from the skies.

THE CALIFORNIA PIONEER.

A pioneer of forty-nine,
  As good as ere came here to mine,
  Or pack around a train
O'er mountain side with pick and pan;
Indeed he was as good a man
  As ever crossed the plain.
He came as others came, to mine for gold;
As other pioneers, the way to mold.

His luck was good, he staked his claim,
For nothing could his purpose maim.
  When dust enough did take
To make a visit to the bay,
Where games and gamesters all did play,
  Inviting all to make
Their games, and now their stakes put down and try;
With clink of gold, then mostly all comply.

They only had the gold to dig
From claims now staked out, small and big,
  And scarcely stopped to count
The value of their bags, well filled,
What matter then if little spilled ?
  To what does it amount ?
For miners then knew where their treasure lay,
As they came back and forward to the bay.

The sport was in the getting same,
To sit at tables, none to blame,
  And pass away the hours.
Perhaps the night might pass away,
And see the morning light so gray
  From Eastern hills, which towers,
Before the miner would give up for rest,
His luck and fortune still did want to test.

What wonder then, in passing time,
There might be what is termed crime,
   When years alone did pass,
No female voices to refine,
No nothing was there in that line,
   But sounds of drinking-glass
To greet the ear in all those days so spent;
At first in nothing but a canvas tent.

This is the way this pioneer,
Through early times and life did peer
   In all the ways of men.
The habits which so long had wrought
Through all those times, also him caught;
   Throughout those years when
He spent in making homes for human race,
Throughout those desert hills and lonesome place.

And cabins which he helped to raise,
For female voice to hear in praise,
   In harmony divine.
The trackless hills of human feet,
No kindred voices did him greet,
   In days of forty-nine.
In all those days this pioneer did spend
To make a home for mankind here and then.

Now twenty years had passed and fled
Since for the sunset traveled Red
   For California life.
And now he has his children five,
His partner, too, she was alive,
   His own dear loving wife,
To comfort him in after life and all,
And him to keep from paths and ways man fall.

He lived as did all pioneers,
Until now getting up in years,
   Had money made enough.
But as with all first comers here,

His time was shortened in this sphere,
  By life so hard and rough.
Then sickened from hard usage, now so tried,
And passed away that pioneer, and died.

Then to another world did go,
As all appear both high and low,
  Now sooner or in late;
And at the gate of paradise
He must appear, he had no choice,
  To see what was his fate.
And as a Californian, lost no time,
But rapped away for entrance there divine.

Then Peter came, and at the gate,
Says, what's the hurry?   What's the State,
  Or country, was your home?
It must a country be that's fast,
Things done in a hurry cannot last;
  And whence now have you come?
Or are you from the earth?   What planet, where?
This hurried rapping I must say is rare.

He answered Peter in this way :
How long would you have me to stay
  An answer for to get?
The place I came from is the earth,
Could send a message round its girth,
  And offered for to bet,
That he could send a message round that globe,
Since he was waiting there without his robe.

Then Peter said, "They're getting smart,
With wondrous ways and cunning art.
  When I was on the earth
It was not known that it was round,
But one continual plain or mound,
  Or that it had a girth;
But now the change is wonderful of late,
Or since I've watched this entrance and this gate."

He asks again, "What part of earth,
Where he had come from, with such worth,
    And rapid motion filled,
And where he spent his early days,
And what he did, and in what ways
    His usefulness distilled,
That he should act so hasty in this sphere,
And come so boldly to these gates up here?"

"America it was my land,
It now is crossed in iron band
    To that Pacific shore;
And California is the name
Of land and State from whence I came.
    I ne'er can see it more;
But if there's resurrection of the dead,
My body still is there, from whence I fled."

Then Peter said, "I thought so, sure;
Whatever hastens or allure,
    Those Californians all,
They come up here with such intent,
I sometimes think they often meant
    To force or scale the wall;
That they could not with patience wait or bear
To ask them whence they came from or from where.

"I cannot let you pass in here;
You must away some other sphere,
    You Californians all;
You are depraved and full of sin,
And nothing can e'er come within
    Who down so low does fall,
And now you must away, and not come back
To ask admittance, for your sins are black."

He stood and looked with full intent
To see and find what Peter meant
    By telling him to go;
Says, "You're the man so little knew

On earth before the cock it crew;
　　When you were down below,
Your Master did deny, and cursed and swore
You never knew the man your burden bore.

"I am of California's line,
A pioneer of forty-nine.
　　My time for years I spent.
Preparing for the world to come
To settle down and make their home,
　　Was still my full intent;
And after twenty years so spent in toil,
I helped to build a city, won't recoil.

I houses built, and church and spire,
Which Christian people still admire;
　　And schools, and temples tall,
And o'er a desert-like frontier
Are settled now, from far and near,
　　Where I went first of all;
There nothing was but sand-hills and a bay:
All this was done in twenty years—what say?

And in the distance very far
It was alone the western star;
　　That country now so large
In population from all climes,
Where I did travel early times,
　　With nothing then in charge,
And everything to work with, bricks and tiles,
By shipping distance nineteen thousand miles.

The tools and all came round Cape Horn,
To build that city from that morn;
　　With tools and all, can say,
The lumber in the forest hills,
Machinery and all the mills,
　　Came round in that same way;
Then distance from the forest trees immense
Had ships to build to ship it there and thence.

Besides the place the city rest
Was the last place to have been blest,
  But long forsaken been
By that Creator of us all,
Who everything both great and small,
  And all creation seen,
For mountains of the sand and drifting wind
Was not inviting—nothing of that kind.

I left that city when in rest;
My body's laid near ocean west,
  Where many a pioneer
Is laid, to sleep his last long sleep
By that Lone Mountain's mound or heap,
  Now watered well with tear;
That city of the dead too grows, alas!
And many a pioneer in here must pass.

You were engaged in catching fish,
And nothing ere had done to wish,
  Nor ought but fish in hauled.
And now you're stationed here so long,
And nothing done but that same song.
  If you had ne'er been called,
You never would been stationed at that gate
To tell a pioneer of such a fate.

But Peter answered that same look,
And from his feet the dust he shook,
  And further off he turned
As not yet ready for to speak.
In silent pause and looking meek,
  As though the whole he spurned.
The pioneer then asked him back to tell,
What he had done on earth deserved so well?

Then Peter said, But all your sins
Are unrepentant, and your kins
  Down where you came from there,
Have gone astray, and all at will,

Unchaste, unsanctified and ill,
  In sin's continual lair,
And nothing enters here unclean from earth,
Or other planets from their home or birth.

Temptations great beset us when
We left our homes and time to spend.
  The early ones at first,
Were all subjected more to sin.
There nothing was that place within,
  And youth for folly thirst,
Were thrown among the fast from everywhere,
Away from grace and gospel, mother's care.

Men did contract those ways they hold,
Which still they have when they grow old,
  Nor could they stand the test.
Those Californians of first run,
First generation to the sun
When setting in the west;
When they came out at first as pioneers,
And left their homes and friends in sorrow's tears.

And led the way to that great west,
Made wealth and homes now for the rest
  Of all mankind to be;
And in the space of twenty years
A rising country young, appears
  In infancy you see;
And at the risk of life and grave sincere,
They should have rest, and all be let in here.

One generation to prepare,
It took from all and everywhere
  That country at that time
For to make ready for the rest,
And down to others their bequest,
  Their country and their clime.
Should all those people then be thrown away?
Was drawn from home, there premature to lay?

They held to god-like doctrine all
Through life, although at times, did fall,
   They die as Christian men.
And all believers promise good,
Which can be said as christian food
   If they repent, and then
Most all in death enjoy the boon, though late,
So now the key put in—unlock that gate.

Then Peter turned again away
And counsel took. He heard him say:
   These Californians all
Come here so persevering now,
There's nothing I can say, I vow,
   When at the gate they call.
And though their sins are scarlet red in stain,
I try to keep them out well nigh in vain.

We might as well at once comply,
And looking round and something sly,
   Says, Pioneer, come in.
And all who left in forty-nine,
And all who of that time and line,
   And all of that first kin;
First generation to that place and shore,
This gate is open!—shall be evermore.

LINES

SENT WIFE WHILE AWAY.

AND now, my dear Maggie, as often I've said,
Since down in that valley, the place we were wed
Where paths then were winding the sand hills around,
And the hills and the valleys as nature was found.

O, you well remember, remember with ease,
The front of that cottage, and two forest trees
Which towered so lofty the cot to defend,
With porch in the center and door on the end.

And you well remember the garden of flowers,
Which opened so blooming in those happy hours,
With sweet scenting fragrance, right under the hill,
Where stood that dear cottage right by the wind-mill.

And then, my dear Maggie, the yard and the shed,
The horse that came to you without e'er been led;
The ducks and the pond, and the dog that did watch
At the gate to come with me when opened the latch.

And, O, our dog Dickey, for that was his name,
I ne'er can forget him, though far from the lane;
How he would come mourning in sorrow and sighs,
When he could not find me, with tears in his eyes.

In sorrow and trouble to you would complain
If he could not find me, and how would remain
In the garden, still mourning in sorrow and tears
If he was not with me, in those happy years.

Would look in your face and with pitiful strain
Beseech you to let him come with me again.
And how he would watch at that entrance and gate
To welcome my coming, both early and late.

What constant affection for me did possess,
And for to come with me how urgent did press;
I ne'er can forget such a faithful, good friend
As was our dog Dickey, until my life's end.

THE FABLE

BETWIXT OCCIDENT AND GOLDSMITH MAID AND LUCY. THE
RESULT OF THE RACES.

IT was on the Pacific shore,
Three thousand miles, it might be more,
  From where the racers stood,
When Occident began to say,
His head aloft, and then did neigh,
  And to himself says, good:
"There's nothing on this coast can make
The time I made, without a break,
  When I am in the mood;
For I went round that course in time and speed
Which tells to all my pedigree and breed.

If I would challenge Goldsmith Maid,
And Lucy, too, I'm not afraid,
  Those mares so proud of flight,
To come and see this distant sphere.
I wonder if they'd laugh and sneer,
  If they would think it right,
To challenge them to cross the plains;
I wonder if they'd take the pains,
  If I would them invite,
If they would make a trip for gold and gear,
Make some excitement in the world out here?

I have been groomed, I have been fed,
I have been drove, I have been led
  In that same way and place,
4

And nothing for my owner made,
My laurels too begin to fade--
   It's music dull to face,
And be the same from day to day,
Monotonous, I now must say,
   To never stretch a trace
With those of a superior race and blood,
This country round the common stock does flood

I feel disgusted here to be,
And nothing noble round me see.
   I'll telegraph to know
If they would like a trip so far
To see me in this western star
   With stock that moves so slow,
And now an answer for to get,
I soon can see how it will set,
   Should it blew high or low;
For to be known and noticed I aspire,
And celebrated be I do admire.

His answer was soon sent and told,
They wished to see the land of gold,
   The sunset and the west,
And try what speed was in his heels.
In admiration now he wheels,
   To have a chance to test
The celebrated trotting mares,
And whom he took nigh unawares.
   And when they have some rest
When they arrive in California's clime,
They'd trot with him, or try it round on time.

The owner of young "Occident"
Began to look with some intent
   On how this thing might pay.
And as he was a railroad man,
He thought it might be a good plan
   To tell without delay,
To have a car arranged to take

For their accommodation make.
  To agents then did say:
To send them through without expense or fares,
Those racers two, with drivers and their mares.

The two fast mares began to make
Remarks upon the time and stake,
  While passing o'er the rail.
While "Goldsmith Maid" began to cough,
And "Lucy" broke in a horse-laugh,
  And stamped and shook her tail,
And female-like, they did begin,
Of "Occident," and of his kin,
  His message sent by mail;
Or how he came to look so far and high,
Of which he may repent, look back and sigh.

The "Maid" replied: It's far, indeed,
To come and try a little speed
  . Of trotting round a park;
And then, with one so little known,
But lately into favor grown;
  Of late but made his mark.
In time, but that is when alone,
And track rolled out as smooth's a stone,
  He feels then gay's a lark.
But when he comes along side of me to score,
I'll harass him so much, he'll want no more.

Then "Lucy" said: As he is young,
He may be fast, and be high strung;
  That is the way to take.
To harass him coquettish-like,
Forget himself, so he may strike,
  And so be wide awake.
And now as you can score the best,
Don't start with him, until you're pressed,
  Then he is sure to break.
As I am oldest, I can tell you truth,
Thus take advantage of his ways and youth.

The " Maid " replies: You've always been
A mother to me when more green;
  I'll always take advice.
When younger I did still adhere
To what you said, and always mere,
  Because you spoke so nice.
I'll do my best, this caution mind,
And when we start he will be blind,
  I'll beat him two in thrice.
By scoring I can work him up, and so
He'l scarcely hear the word to start or go.

Then " Lucy " said: When I go round
The course with him he must be sound,
  For I am firm and strong.
I'll let him dart ahead; he must;
And to my strength I then can trust
  In coming home among
The crowds of people who will go
To see the race, from high to low.
  In that promiscuous throng
I'll put myself to work with my whole strength,
And then I'll pass him home at least one length.

'Twas all arranged how they would take,
And thus how they could win the stake
  And carry off the prize.
Then won't they feel so cheap and blue
To have him beat by both us two?
  If we so work it wise
And cunning, for there's more in that.
And now I say and tell you what,—
  And here they both did rise
Unto their feet, for they were both in bed,—
And looking round say, Time that we were fed.

Thus day by day the mares did make
Their minds up how they'd win the stake,
  When at their journey's end;

And their engagements well did keep,
Although fatigue and loss of sleep
  Did no assistance send.
"Now for a few days' resting spell,
So we may feel ourselves as well,
  Before we do attend,
To run the first race o'er the track with him,"
Whom they found dark and looking very trim.

Then for the race the day was set,
For Goldsmith Maid to win the bet;
  She watched him very clear.
Near dozen times now with him scored;
She kept her strength together stored,
  When he came close or near.
At last got off, he shot ahead,
She overtook and now him led,
  He sweating now with fear.
She passed and came toward the winning post,
While pools and bets stood two to one at most.

The second heat: now for a start;
The Maid again, coquettish art,
  In coming to the score,
Came dashing, and then checked her speed,
To fool that nimble-footed steed,
  The same as done before,
Until the horse began to fret,
And says, "We never off will get,
  My patience out is wore
With ways of that coquettish Goldsmith Maid;
I only wish she was more staunch and staid."

They get away as with a rush,
And for the heat the horse did push
  For the half mile, and lo!
The horse ahead in rapid stride;
The Maid comes up in maiden pride,
  And closes on him so.

Now she steps out towards the pole,
So all can see her as a whole
　　How fast she now can go.
This heat she also wins and him she led,
While Occidental faces now were red.

The third heat now was called again;
He wants to go with might and main.
　　The race it was so set,
Best three in five, it was the rule;
He calls himself an ass or mule,
　　If this heat he don't get.
So she won't boast of every heat
O'er this great land of gold and wheat,
　　He now begins to fret.
They start again: this time will tell the whole;
The same as other two—she past him stole.

The last heat round the course was run,
Within one hour of setting sun,
　　On Sacramento track.
Then many left and went their way,
For Occident had lost the day,
　　Too late to bring it back.
There is one other racer near,
They both came on to run out here;
　　To try again won't lack.
"I'll surely pass that awful clumsy mare,
Who looks so old and built so strong and square."

The match again was made to be
Now at a place where near the sea,
　　Across the spreading Bay
Of San Francisco to the east,
Alameda Park, to say the least,
　　It's on the railroad way,
Not far from where the ferry end,
So all can now the race attend,
　　And meet with no delay.
The day was coming now when they must try
For Occident reverse the hue and cry.

The tickets and the pools were sold,
The morning came with storm and cold,
  Some rain had blown and fell
Upon the course, which made all say
The race will not come off to-day,
  Which any one can tell.
Some went across in storm and rain,
But soon found out it was in vain;
  The race put off as well
Until some other day when weather clear,
Not far away, but some time very near.

The weather fine, the day was fixed
For all to go here so much mixed,
  The race to see did vow.
And then away in boat loads went,
To see the race now all was bent,
  And time all did allow
Themselves to cross the bay and see
That race so—so long that was to be,
  This day and place and now.
In thousands crowded on the boats and cars;
The rich and poor, and some were jolly tars.

The track now enters " Occident."
On seeing him, she to him sent
  A look of half disdain;
Says, That's the celebrated horse?
Before he's three times round this course,
  Or ere we do refrain,   ◆
My strength and speed he's sure to feel.
To score and start they now did wheel,
  Get off now like a train.
In railroad speed they went the first half mile,
And he ahead now shot, thus far in style.

She stretching out to end the joke,
And coming up on him he broke.
  Before he had regained

His speed in trotting, she was gone
Ahead of him.   Now left alone,
    Then to come up he feigned,
But was too late to overtake,
Or for to cure that ugly break
    And loss he had sustained.
She, coming.in some lengths ahead at ease,
Enjoying now whatever gait she pleased.

The second heat again called up,
But "Occident" did sorrow sup.
    When off they went on run;
As usual, "Occident" ahead.
She coming up, raised the old Ned,
    As though she liked the fun;
For coming near him, to enhance,
The music played, which made him dance,
    His folly then did shun;
And coming in full speed, left him behind,
To dance away, as long's as he had mind.

And bye and bye, came home alone,
So distanced now, the race was done.
    And homeward now all must;
When one and all say, What a farce !
To get away now, from the course,
    All turned in disgust,
And feeling tame, with a long face,
Say, What a humbug ! What a race!
    And looking in distrust,
All felt as though they had been sold; and now,
It was the last race they would see, did vow.

Now for the city took the lead,
The leading men, in railroad speed,
    In haste to get away.
And out of sight they all partook,
And with a glance, and with a look,
    Never passed the time of day

To one another, as on 'change;
Nor did one syllable exchange,
　　But home without delay,
For to themselves to ponder and to think:
To my expense, add one other link.

To tell the number now was sold,
Of youth and beauty, and the old,
　　And millionaires, that day,
Which "Occident" together drew,
And fooled, and left them in a stew,
　　Is rather hard to say.
Ten thousand ! Might be more, or less,
A Yankee would be sure to guess;
　　All looking in array
To see the horse or Occidental dance,
In something new, which never came from France.

A child on mother's lap did sit,
This question asked in infant wit:
　　While man and horse did fill,
And as away their horses turned,
As though such folly now they spurned;
　　And says in child-like will,
What horses, mother, runs the race ?
Or where's the horses and the place ?
　　Is that them on the hill,
Which runs so fast together in a band
Upon yon mountain tops and o'er the land ?

The mares, now stabled side by side,
Began again to laugh out wide
　　About the horse's run,
And was some time before they should
Get out one word or e'er they could
　　Get through their laugh and fun.
They laughed themselves hysteric near,
Till from their eyes did start a tear,
　　And when they had begun,

Or circumspect become, or word did make,
Their very heads and hearts and sides did ache.

Then when they had got through or calm,
Their fun to them was quite a balm,
   For all their travels west;
And now to sober solid thought
Of him whom they had brought to naught,
   And at his own request,
To come out here, made so polite
For both of us he did invite;
   We came at his behest;
And now excuse of fright for folly feigns,
His trainer blames, or man who held the reins.

Then Lucy said, "I am a judge
Of horse flesh, and I don't begrudge
   His owner of his stock,
For no one knows his pedigree;
There's one thing we all can see,
   In which there is no mock,
His head and neck a mixture is
Of mustang race ;" then with a quiz,
   At that the Maid did shock.
There is a spark of that cross race out here,
You cannot well depend to for the'll shear.

The Maid looked up—says, "That is so;
For in his neck is little bow,
   But as a donkey's stand
Out from his shoulders donkey-like;
The first thing to which me did strike
   When I came to this land,
For when I met him the first time,
I noticed that, though in his prime,
   His neck it was so planned.
I don't believe his pedigree is pure,
Or that he from a noble race inure.

" He may run off a little while,
Perhaps it may be half a mile,
　　And then may either break
Or make some other blunder so;
Which no one e'er can in him know,
　　Into his head will take,
And just enough to not be sure
Of him, and something none can cure
　　Or ever better make.
Just see how he went with us, broke and danced,
And fairly up and down he jumped and pranced."

He fooled the Californians all,
But money made the railroads all;
　　His owner he paid well,
And as he is a railroad man,
To lose the race he well can stand,
　　Which every one can tell.
But when he makes another race
For to come off in that same place,
　　To charm the rich in spell,
And California's name and fame sustain,
Some other kind of horses he will train.

LINES

WRITTEN ON JAMES KING OF WILLIAM, AT THE TIME AND
SPIRIT OF THE STARTING OF THE "SAN FRANCISCO
BULLETIN."

HAIL to our chieftain brave!
　　Ne'er yet à cringing slave!
　　Him let us sing.
Now let the wreath be bound
With garland roses round,
And let our chief be crowned,
　　Always our King!

When here the right was chained,
And dark corruption reigned
　　Spread on the wing,
Who did the fetters break ?
Through ravines, hills and lake,
Calling to duty, wake,
　　Who but our King ?

Welcome then, comes the sheet,
Which reformation seek,
　　Fearless to bring
On moral suasion's rod,
On those, who down have trod,
On the best works of god,
　　Honesty,—King !

Truth still upon your side,
And let what will betide,
　　Far may it ring
Till all this favored land
Joins with you, heart and hand.
All in a happy band.
　　God save our King !

LINES ON GRANDMOTHER McQUEEN.

SHE'S eighty-five now, every year,
With those black eyes still looking clear.
　　How seldom do we find
In people of her age the will
To do, and duty to fulfill
　　In memory and mind.

So perfect; and she still aspires
To duty, which she still admires.
　　As years through life was spent

In place where women most belong,
As mother, and amid the throng
   And place for women meant.

With ardent wish and zealous will,
Her home and place so long did fill,
   And never discontent.
But still the same her friends among,
Ne'er out of place those years so long,
   Through life of duty bent.

The table with its daily bread,
How often by those hands been spread
   In days now past and gone?
Which vanished with the flight of time,
Those days when in her youth and prime,
   Has vanished one by one.

The form once cast by Nature's mold,
No imperfection on it told,
   Though time may shrink away.
But spirit never can be less,
Has seen those days which few possess,
   The time is short we stay.

For Time is ever on the wing,
And with him all that change must bring
   Which passes o'er our fate.
There nothing is but Time compels
To succumb to long years and spells
   In sooner or in late.

THE CONCEPTION OF WRONG.

HOW often do the blemish
   Those ways conceived as harm,
In giving that conception
   Which always does unarm,
Impotent ways engenders,
   And health and life annoys,
Through life, in dire disturbance,
   And usefulness destroys.

By that conceived by mortals,
   Or fellow-creatures here,
To be of such transgression
   On this terrestial sphere,
As never can be pardoned,
   Or mercy ever find,
Which poisons all life's fountains,
   And always in the mind.

O, happy for creation,
   For man through life, and all,
Was never conceived as evil,
   That mentioned by the fall;
Which filled life's cup o'erflowing
   With wormwood and with gall,
By being conceived as evil,
   That mentioned by that fall.

SAN FRANCISCO SUMMER WINDS.

THROUGH city and State,
Through that deep Golden Gate
Where the ocean in force, ebb and flows
   To her wide spreading bay,
   Where the steamers do play,
How the western breezes, still blow.

   Through streets, and her lanes,
   And her arteries' mains,
Making pure all the places so low
   With her pure cooling breath;
   Where the emblems of death
Move in mystery round, to and fro.

   O'er mountains in shrouds,
   Where the fog rolls in clouds
O'er the hills and the valleys so low,
   With your pure cooling blast,
   From that ocean so vast,
Where in majesty still ebbs and flow.

   What would all be for thee,
   Thou great glorious sea,
With thy cool blowing winds o'er us cast,
   O'er our city so grand
   As she now takes a stand,
But thy pure and thy sea-cooling blast..

NEW VERSION OF HOME AGAIN.

WRITTEN TO MRS. HENSHELWOOD, WHILE MAKING A RURAL
SUMMER VISIT IN SANTA CLARA VALLEY IN TIME OF THE
SAN FRANCISCO SUMMER WINDS.

COME home again, home again,
  Near that great ocean's shore.
O, how it fills the soul with joy,
  To meet our friends once more.
            Home again.

Home again, home again,
  Where winds and fogs roll o'er,
And sand-hills drift with clouds of dust,
  Come home, come home, once more
            Home again.

Happy thoughts, happy thoughts,
  To think of that sweet home,
Where clouds of fog and sand roll o'er,
  To greet you when you come
            Home again.

Home again, home again,
  From Santa Clara's vale,
Where garden flowers are in full bloom
  To sand-hills, bare and stale,
            Home again.

Come home again, home again,
  Where domes and spires and towers
Here still ascend among the clouds,
  And husbands keep good hours.
            Home again.

ON PASSING SUNDAY, JUNE 22D, 1873, IN SAN FRANCISCO.

ON Sunday morning, while we sat,
  The teapot on the tray or mat,
While Maggie held the handle tight,
And tried to pour with all her might
  From teapot large and brown,
And coffee, for we had our choice,
To ask it with becoming voice,
  And thinking of this town,
And of its hills and valleys and the rest,
And Golden Gate, that key to all the west.

One of our circle did propose
To see the western hills and those
Of northern decline to view,
And as perchance see something new;
  Our number was just four.
We sallied out, the morning clear,
And feeling good from breakfast cheer,
  And passing round the gour,
And for the car passed up the sloping hill;
The sky was clear, the morning air not chill.

Our names you well can guess and tell,
Indeed they are not hard to spell;
Three letters for each name will sound
What we will answer to all round.
  And here I will make known
And tell what letters make the space,
So you can know our names and place;
  We long have been men grown.
The first one's name is Uncle Tom for him,
The next one's Uncle Joe, then Bob, then Jim.

We reached the car and all got in,
And hoped it might not be a sin,

When wives away, to look at those
Who sat there blooming as a rose,
   ' And never thinking ill
Of those who might look round perchance,
And at the same time take a glance,
   In winding round the hill.
Where sometimes speed was doubled round the curve,
And as to try the strength of horse and nerve.

The harbor reached, and now to see,
And ocean beach along to be.
The sight was beautiful to look,
A dozen sail, which all partook,
   Through wind and wave to steer
For distant ports with ebbing tide,
Soon vanished for the ocean wide;
   Though looking first so near,
Yet soon they passed away and out of sight
For that great ocean wave in all its might.

The narrow entrance at the fort
Prevents the sea from making sport
With her long ocean wave at times,
Which runs so long in dashing lines
   For shore or beach amain;
But soon finds out those solid rocks
Her line of battle only mocks,
   Though she should come again;
Those craggy pillars long the war did wage,
And in convulsion throw her billows' rage.

The heavy rolling of the wave,
Like that deep sound some organs gave,
In tones so low in awe did keep
Us listening to their moans so deep,
   And to the spell was bound,
While listening to their hollow strains,
Which tells a great Creator reigns,
   Was whispered in the sound
Which round this world's circuit never dies,
Still mingles with the winds in solemn sighs.

But time was passing on so fast,
A look towards our home we cast;
For when we left we promised to
Back to dinner just at two.
    Then for the horse and rail;
Now in the car, the horses start,
But one of them he had the art
    Of thrashing like a flail
Upon the dasher with his feet behind,
Which, lucky for the driver, was well lined.

But off he goes, and as for fun,
And up the hill as by the run;
Then stops again and backs us down;
Then looking back, half turning round,
    Thinks, "Now I am all right;
To face that hill I cannot think,
Attached to traces and this link;"
    And tried with all his might
To keep his head still turned towards the beach,
And still refused the traces for to stretch.

Still patiently the driver hooked,
He turned his head and then he looked,
And thought it don't look now so steep,
And then he bounded with a leap;
    How soon he topped the hill,
And with him took more than his share.
And on the hill did pant and stare,
    Thinks now I am at will
To stop or go again, I'll make my mind;
The driver still to him was very kind.

Till horse and driver did agree,
An emblem on a bunch of three,
'Twas not the shamrock nor the rose,
But thistle, as you might suppose,
    Discovered all alone,
Was taken trimmed for Maggie Ross,

By James, so she would not feel cross
   In being late from home,
Or dinner waiting by a baulky horse,
Again to meet more temper still was worse.

But dinner in good time was struck,
Which told us that we were in luck.
We sat, for now our appetite
Was whispering not to be polite,
   But eat in haste and will.
And when we justice done the plates,
It was agreed that we, as mates,
   Would hear the pilgrim still;
That Singing Pilgrim with melodious voice,
And now the Tabernacle made our choice.

The time on Sunday evening, same
As other churches, now had came.
It now was lit and looking fine,
Those seats, which circle in a line,
   Their way the people willed
From everywhere, in every door,
Came down the aisles and steps and floor,
   Until the house was filled.
The pastor coming to his seat, and when,
Gave out the page to sing from, thence and then.

All nearly joined in songs of praise,
Regardless of their worldly ways;
But, O! the discord was so grand,
The ocean's voice, o'er rocks and sand,
   Was music to the ear,
Compared to some with voices gone,
By age and care, perhaps alone
   With worldly cares and fear,
Their voices grating, some on different notes,
In a harsh sound, while through the air it floats.

The minister said, Let us pray.
They all agreed, for none said nay;

They bowed consent to have it so.
He was the only one did know
   The prayer he now would say.
But earnestly he did appeal,
His supplication they might feel,
   On this same night and day;
That sinners would confess their sins, and come,
And that converted be this night might some.

They sung once more, and then to preach—
To tell them how that heaven to reach,
And never wait convenient space,
Convenient season, time, or place,
   The blessing for to find.
And never more the Spirit scoff;
No. longer for to put it off,
   The Scripture's teachings mind.
In very fervent words and earnest care,
To do what God requires while He forbear.

The singing pilgrim then in strains
Of silver chord, while silence reigns
Throughout the circle, large and calm,
To all it acted as a balm;
   And when his tones out died,
Suspended animation reigned,
Until to break the silence feigned,
   Inviting all he tried
To join with him in hearty, fervent song,
That congregation circling round in throng.

To join they did, with all their might;
But that same jar and discord's flight
From many voices different pitch
On different notes—ne'er thought of which
   Would harmonize so well.
The tune on minor key was set,
Which made it harder for to get
   In harmony of swell,

Besides, the hymn was very dry and long,
The music died towards the end of song.

"Praise God, from whom all blessings flow,"
Was sung by all, both high and low,
For ages past and gone so far,
In harmony, without a jar
    Was sung with voices here.
And those from churches often stay,
And very seldom ever pray
    From every land and sphere,
When that familiar music broke sublime,
Was made to join in praises still divine.

LINES

WRITTEN ON HEARING OF THE DEATH OF AN ESTIMABLE
FRIEND, CHARACTERISTIC OF A VALUABLE AND GOOD MAN.

O HOW can I realize what has been read,
    Or how can we think that the good man is dead?
Is there no mistake in this saddest of news?
Is anxious inqnired as the word here diffuse.
The distance is far and the name may be rared
Of some one which died who might be better spared.
But no; here's a letter, the words emphasized.
O, must it be certain or now realized
That one so beloved and respected has gone?
If so, then Great Parent, Thy will must be done,
For all here must succumb to death's stern decree;
It is so with you and it is so with me.

The life he has yielded is to Nature's law,
For laws true to Nature a child in him saw;
How natural, then, for a child thus to yield

To parent who loved him and chose him to shield
From paths with unrighteousness fearful and rife.
Through his short space of time, but useful spent life,
As father and parent to one and to all,
Who looked for protection or on him would call;
Advice for protection, his heart and his hand
Alike was to all and the poor of the land,
And no compensation, alas, could expect—
The act in itself compensation direct.
And happy he must been, still cheerful him find,
Reversed to all cruelty, whatever kind;
Forbearance with creatures how often would crave,
An old pioneer as a friend of the slave;
Indeed, in advance of his day and his time,
But mantle successful is dropped now sublime
On a country beloved, now arising in peace,
From the dark stain of which he so longed to efface.

How many looked up to the best of all men,
And many endearments about him could pen,
As always beseeching so earnest and plain,
From all that intoxicates surely abstain.
There's many now blest by this fatherly guide,
And many look back on his time now with pride,
When followed him on to it seemed then afar
To the land of the free as the pioneer star.
Now follow in death we are sure and we must;
'Tis so with the wicked, 'tis so with the just.
'Tis said in the Scriptures, authority best,
The merciful here is with mercy still blest.
If so, then the one who has gone from all sight;
With that, as in all things, was found in the right,
For years now gone past and the time now unrolled
Reveals but a part and the half can't be told
His goodness on earth, but now gone to his rest,
Great Spirit, now hovering along with the blest.

But though he has gone, it is mete to proceed
A little advance and the way for to lead

Through death's dreadful portals and way to the tomb,
And soften the way so much shaded in gloom.
From which no one ever came back for to tell
Of myriads who's gone to say what them befell;
Or if they were better than here upon earth,
From when they departed till day of their birth.
But God, the great Source of all infinite things,
Sees good will and pleasure in all which he brings
To pass upon earth, or this planet of ousr,
From which men's cut down like the grass or the flowers.

But still he is living, I can't think him dead,
Although his great spirit from earth may have fled.
For still in ourselves we discover his ways,
As the sun o'er the landscape in shedding his rays,
A cloud may arise and cut off her anew,
The brilliance of which is now lost to the view;
But still the effect of the sun's genial beams
O'er the landscape and earth, the watering streams,
Is felt o'er the wildest of Nature's own hills,
The genial effect of the shower she distills;
Through landscape and valleys is felt still sublime,
Through all Nature's fountains and various clime.
So is the effect of the mind upon mind;
On minds not so fertile how often we find
Ourselves those same symptoms prone to imitate
The great man, by nature the only man great.
Indeed, we will not imitate the learned man,
Through grave looking aspect or student so wan,
Through deep-thinking research or fathomless ways,
Where natural sunbeams near sheds forth her rays;
But where Nature's fountain still ready to flow
For all fellow-creatures, no matter how low,
Belongs the true goodness by natural cast,
Which worthy of all things and always to last.

And if he has left here, and race may have run,
His spirit's transcended from father to son,
And time and the future are sure to restore,

Like spirit which left us and fled evermore;
But, O, it was cruel for Death on his way
Not spare him a while little longer to stay,
Enjoy the sweet fruits of an industrious hand
So honestly reaped from this much favored land.
Cut off at a time, and his life had to give
When just as he might think him ready to live.
Now who will we look to for fatherly care,
If he has now left us, or who will now share
Our troubles and sorrows, with whom here below,
When heart full of sorrow now where shall we go?
The loss is a great one, the hand and the rod
Which laid the affliction, but all is with God.

THE GRAVES OF THE PATRIOTS, BAKER AND THOMAS STARR KING.

THE deep sounding roar of that ocean,
  Strikes over the hills to the ear,
And whispers the depth of emotion,
    And moistens the ground with a tear
      For the dead near her shore,
      Which can never no more
      Be awoke from repose;
      For all silent are those
Who are laid near the side of her crest—
Laid in peace in the far distant West.

How many are laid there reposing
  Their graves and their monuments tell,
Their lands and their ages disclosing,
    And names with their nations as well;
      And the marble relate
      Where the great men of State
      Sleep beneath its cold face,
      And the spot where to trace

5

Where they laid them away at their rest,
Near the shores of the far distant West.

Where BAKER is quietly sleeping,
  Who died for his country to save,
The dewdrops of ocean are weeping,
  Distilled on the tablet and grave;
    Drops, as tears on the sands,
    Where no monuments stands,
    On that sacred spot,
    Looking nearly forgot
By his country, for which he bestowed
His pure life's blood, on which it has flowed.

The grave of a KING is in hearing
  The sound of that great ocean's roar,
As it moves through the air, still revering
  Its maker in deep sounding lore.
    But that evening strain
    Of that deep rolling main
    Never more can he hear;
    Or his mellow voice clear
Ever tell of her organ's great song,
Or the music, her shores all along;

For laid in that sepulchre slumber,
  Reposing in death's solemn dream,
How quickly his days they were numbered,
  While passing down life's fickle stream,
    And his loss was the more,
    To a country he bore
    Through her trials so vast,
    For her destiny cast,
With his eloquent voice for to stand
By the flag of their country and land.

When drifting on rocks which might sever,
  With crew from all nations on hand,
Not knowing her fate, or if ever
  She would reach her destiny's land.

How the sound of his voice
Made his people rejoice,
And inspired all to stand
By the flag of their land ;
And a sister State, though she was young,
Keep her place with her sisters among.

The pure patriot's words all admired,
  To save this great Union in strength,
All this people and State he inspired,
  Throughout its great size and its length.
    In her people suppressed,
    Of that spirit possessed,
    Of the right to secede
    Which they then did concede,
By the power of his patriot will,
And that eloquent voice now so still.

In his church-yard now stands all alone
  The marble to show where he rests;
'Neath his chapel as monument stone,
  For that was his will and request.
    While that liberal mind
    Will that charity find,
    His great spirit possessed,
    Which has gone to its rest,
And his liberal doctrine is found
To encircle this planet all round.

His memory still with emotion
  His people still cherish so dear,
And often, in silent devotion
  Is moistened the eye with a tear
    When that name 's mentioned o'er,
    Is still sure to restore
    Recollections and time,
    When his voice so sublime,
In those eloquent strains did arise
Irrepressible, prudent, and wise.

LINES

WRITTEN AT THE DEATH-BED OF THE AUTHOR'S NEICE, WHO
DIED OF CONSUMPTION.

THE day star of life is still waning,
  The flickering light still is feigning
    To pierce through the gloom
Of the distance, but weaker,
Still weaker, but meeker;
    The time to go out must be soon.

The sunshine of life disappearing,
The noon-time of life, though so cheering,
    Is passing away.
The rose-bud of life was but blooming,
The lifetime of youth was but nooning,
    When sapped by the worm of decay.

The foe of all earth's habitation
Struck low, at the very foundation,
    With aim that was sure.
And sapping the veins of life's glowing,
All hopes for the future o'erthrowing,
    And hoping was but to allure.

The stream of life's ebbing and flowing,
But lower and weaker she's growing,
    And passing away.
The husband, long patient in watching,
Each word from her last, low words catching,
    Won't have her long with him to stay.

Dear mother, your daughter is dying,
The time is now short, and is flying,
    And father I fear—
Come near, for my breathing's oppressing;
Come near me, and give me your blessing,
    And tell all my sisters, come near.

But don't let me die without bringing
My baby, who round my bed clinging
 In infant-like charms;
The curling hair she possesses,
These skeleton hands made those tresses,
 When on my knee sitting in arms.

And friends, and relations, and brother,
I'll bid you adieu for another
 Sphere, distant to come;
For dying is only the giving,
Or sowing the seeds of the living,
 Which blooms in the garden of home.

LONE MOUNTAIN.

THAT mountain looks lonely and lonesome at best;
 No wonder they named it Lone Mountain
As it stands on the verge of the far distant west;
In its bosom how many a pioneer rest
 In their graves, in that still, quiet mountain?

The surface is carved, and all points to the skies;
 Those monuments stand by that mountain,
For to tell where the men from all nations now lies,
And that many have died from their kindred and ties,
 In their graves in this far distant mountain.

The glittering gold-fields so near to the sun
 When setting behind that Lone Mountain;
But reflections of placers so far now begun,
Holding forth such inducements, which many have run
 But to sleep in their graves in Lone Mountain.

The young and the venturesome, bold and so brave,
 Once home far away from that mountain.
In the prime of their manhood all doubting must waiv,

For enchanting the distance, in many a cave
  Lays the treasure still hid, near that mountain.

The color is yellow, and nothing to fear,
  In land so far west, near that mountain.
As the farmer and craftsman, with many a tear,
Left their children so small, and their wife to them d ear
  But to rest in that far distant mountain.

And the man with rich talents, his mind on the place,
  Still westward inclines to that mountain,
For the sunsets so yellow, he cannot efface
From his mind, though himself is the pride of his race,
  But he must see the land near that mountain.

Now great growing city, so near to the gate,
  Arising so grand near that mountain,
Which the living feel proud of, but just contemplate
Of the growth of that city, which hard to relate,
  Grows as fast with the dead in Lone Mountain.

They hail from all countries and climes upon earth,
  As laid by the foot of Lone Mountain.
And the monuments tell of the men of great worth,
And place where they come from, and place of their
    birth.
  Now asleep by the side of Lone Mountain.

There sleeps the pure patriots, Baker and King,
  In sepulchre laid near that mountain.
To their eloquent voices, how memory cling,
And those words touched, inspired by an angelic wing,
  Ne'er more to be heard near Lone Mountain.

And there sleeps the dead, who as students of will,
  Graced surgery's aid near that mountain,
And who stood at the head as Professor and skill,
Always ready to aid the unfortunate still,
  But now gone to their graves, in Lone Mountain.

How many a student in medicine test
  Is laid to repose in that mountain ?
Where no call can awake them, or patient's request
Can disturb their deep sleep, for they have found a rest
  Ne'er disturbed or awoke, in Lone Mountain.

Their monuments' shafts rises high to relate
  From hill looking west to that mountain;
And to tell where a Broderick, or great man of State,
Lies still in its bosom, who met with his fate
  For his country, now laid in Lone Mountain.

The clear, mellow voice, is now hushed in repose,
  In tribunal courts, near that mountain,
Where so often in eloquent strains has arose
In the hearing of judges and jurors, and those
  Of a Byrne, now asleep, near Lone Mountain.

They are all now at rest, where the eloquent sound
  Of ocean is heard, near that mountain;
Where she outward and inward, unceasing bound,
Ne'er resting at ease, as the dead all around,
  In their graves by the side of Lone Mountain.

The sound of her voice, as her children's asleep,
  In whispering tones near that mountain,
And as though in a lullaby, quiet would keep,
Or the silence which death makes when moved for to
    weep,
  She displays for her dead in Lone Mountain.

What matter it now to the still, quiet dead,
  Though rage as she may, near that mountain ?
But how vast is the contrast, no sound or a tread
Since released from their anguish, or from a death bed,
  Is e'er heard by the side of Lone Mountain.

No place upon earth, for the dead to repose,
  More suitable is than that mountain,

Where the requiem music still chanting for those,
And the winds from that ocean, her anthem disclose
   For repose of the dead in Lone Mountain.

The cross lifted np to the top of the mount,
   As signal of agony's fountain,
To the world and the living, to show what a fount,
Giving manifestation to all what account
   They are of, by the side of Lone Mountain.

Through thick and dense fogs, comes the tones of the
    bell,
   In moans o'er the sand-hills and mountain,
And it mingles that same solemn note for to tell,
With that voice from the ocean still chanting as well,
   For repose of the dead in Lone Mountain.

Sleep on then, what better can Nature do more
   For repose of the dead in Lone Mountain?
Than to sing through the winds of that great ocean's
    roar,
For the dead, now reposing not far from her shore,
   Ne'er to wake until called from Lone Mountain.

ON RECOLLECTIONS

OF HEARING FATHER TAILOR PREACH A SERMON TO THE SAIL-
ORS IN THE OLD BETHEL CHURCH, NORTH SQUARE, BOSTON.

THE flag-staff was waving its banner that hour
So playfully round from that old Bethel tower;
And playful it fluttered, and proud seemed to be,
The pride of the brave, in the land of the free.

The day was the Sabbath, and called by the bell,
The church-going people, the seamen as well,
Had come from the distance, away from afar,
To hear of the tidings of Bethelem Star.

Her gates thrown open, so wide to afford,
That plain, hallowed temple, was free to His word,
While faithful's the watchman on Zion's fair wall,
Still faithful to duty, attends to his call.

He enters her gates, and ascends to his post,
For beauteous Zion, her walls he loves most;
He opens the book, and commences to read,
With voice still so mellow, and earnest indeed.

The hymn so sincerely, and words read so clear,
Which swelled the great heart of the seamen to hear,
While sweet sounds of music came murmuring forth,
Reminding the sailor the place of his birth.

Then fervent in prayer he did earnestly kneel,
The great supplication so earnest they feel;
Then opened the Gospel, in love did proceed
The mind of the mariner now for to lead.

In calls for the sinner to hear the bequest
Of pardoning grace from their sins now to rest.
"O, turn you ! O, turn you !" in tears he did cry;
My Master and Captain he also asks why.

Shall the bosom of love in vain bear the loss
Of a well beloved Son to be nailed to the cross?
Forbid it, great Captain; thy mercy we seek,
While tears found deep channels to course down his
    cheek.

The heart of the mariner swelled to the cry,
And few were in hearing, but tears dimmed their eye;
But now he has gone from that plain hallowed spot
The way of all flesh and the way and the lot.

He has crossed o'er the stream, in safety he rides,
Safe anchored from winds, or the eddies, or tides,
Or the whirlpools of life, uncertain at best,
Enjoying a peaceful repose with the blest.

How often in rapture he looked to the skies,
To tell to the seamen, with tears in his eyes,
The place where to anchor, his chart in his hand,
The Bible his chart, by Divinity planned.

Of Bethlehem Star and the wise men of old,
That plan of redemption how often he's told,
To seamen and landsmen from distance afar,
How often has told of that Bethlehem Star.

ERR ON THE SIDE OF MERCY.

ERR on the side of mercy,
    If err we must at all;
Imperfect all in judgment,
    In error we must fall.

Imperfect in our judgments,
    Imperfect one and all,
But let us err in mercy,
    In error we must fall.

If error, still 'tis noble
  If mercy we incline,
And scale is turned by mercy
  In making up our mind.

That creature siill is noble
  His fellow-men among,
If still inclines to mercy
  And fears he might be wrong.

His fellow-man condemning,
  Like error he is prone,
And must receive same mercy
  When at the judgment throne.

For who can sit in judgment,
  Or tell the inmost thought,
Or that which was promoter
  Of error which him caught.

His mind made weak by nature,
  So often overcome
By promptings strong to error,
  Which bred and born in some.

That mercy still is wanting,
  Can see through good and bad,
Alike through all creation,
  The joyful and the sad.

For all is good through nature,
  Ne'er altered is her law,
Fixed as the earth and ocean
  Before the light we saw.

Those laws were given nature,
  She ne'er could violate,
So that which will befall us,
  Whatever is our fate.

All to those laws must succumb,
   The consequence what may;
All must fulfill her dictates—
   No one can e'er say nay.

Till all alike she makes us
   By death in silent sleep,
She makes for to pass o'er us,
   No more in trouble weep.

Then all receive that mercy
   Which felt among the blest,
All subject to same judgment
   To others they behest.

Then all incline to mercy,
   In error all must fall;
There's no such thing as perfect
   On this terrestrial ball.

The very air uncertain
   We breathe, made so by change,
While all the earth is changing,
   To all its center range.

Her veins are cold and chilly,
   At others hot and warm;
At times burst forth in fury,
   In terrible alarm.

And then her sea and oceans
   At times in awful rage,
And then so calm and gentle,
   When anger does assuage.

Her climate and her nature,
   We all to earth belong,
Her nourishment partaking,
   As parent all among.

Her mountains and her valleys
  To that same mother cling,
As infant in its nursing,
  Our nourishment she bring.

And all of that same nature
  Which changes through all time,
At times in rage and frenzy,
  May end in haste and crime.

And all inclined by nature,
  By that same way and change,
As mother earth herself is,
  Which nature's laws arrange.

And then in hasty moments
  The promptings don't withstand,
Act out her lawful dictates,
  And by her own command.

Then God may help the victim
  By passion made a wreck,
Acts out what can't be undone,
  But still remains a speck.

Upon the name, and nothing
  Can blot that speck or stain,
Although it's Nature's impress,
 · Forever it remain.

The world it leaves a frowning
  On them where'r they be;
Themselves she leaves reproaching,
  But never can get free.

Then life itself is poisoned,
  While all of nature teems
With life's pure flowing fountains
  And her pure running streams.

And nothing left but bitter,
 Or streams which never pure,
But galling thoughts reproachful
 For that which did allure.

That mercy still is wanting,
 Can see through good and bad,
Alike through all creation,
 The joyful and the sad.

Then all incline to mercy,
 And blot a brother's stain;
From mother earth he nursed it,
 And from our mother's vein.

LINES

ON THE AUTHOR'S WIFE, WHO DIED OF CONSUMPTION IN BOSTON.

O MARY, how can I now think of the time
 Or the days of our youth now gone past,
When creation and life in those days then sublime,
 Which soon faded and gone from us fast?
Those days when at longest then endless would seem,
But now all has gone past and it seems but a dream.

Those days when you looked for the night for to come,
 And the time when you watched from the floor
How my footsteps you knew in the distance from home,
 Long before I had come to the door,
Those days still how quickly they all passed away,
And how short was the time when we wished it to stay.

Those days I won't think of, I cannot well try,
 And besides they have gone now so far,
But will just take a glimpse at the time now gone by,

Is the most I can do, as the star
Of life is at noontime—before it gets past,
I will take a last look, for it may be the last.

We lived and we loved, my dear May, too well;
  It was wicked an idol to make
Of each other the reason that what us befell,
  When to leave you I did for your sake;
But thinking my fortune to better in land,
And again to return to my Mary was planned.

We parted—how well I remember the time:
  Bid adeiu to the children so small,
For the land where the treasure and gold and the clime
  Was enchanting and ready for all;
Arriving in distance from perilous way,
Where I tried all I could for to shorten my stay.

But distance was far for my Mary to live,
  And she longed for to live as before;
For the time was so long that she could not well give,
  And she wanted me home all the more.
I wrote of the place: if she would she might come
To the land of much promise and make us a home.

She came, and our cottage was near to the hill,
  Where we lived with our children four;
But the delicate flower, which the harsh winds do ill,
  And which chill to the heart and the core—
They came with that blight which strikes withering decay.
Left but death, which was certain and fading away.

My Mary we laid in that tomb by the pond
  Where it circles all round with a fence,
And my heart still is bleeding for her who so fond
  Lived for me, with so little pretense.
She's laid in that tomb by the pond or the lake,
In the still sleep of death, where no winds can awake.

She lies in that cold house of death far from here,
  Where the cold Eastern winters still pass,
Where the harsh and cold winds never trouble or fear
  Or the delicate flower more. harass;
The flower was too delicate for to withstand,
And it was but transplanted to climate or land

More suitable, where the harsh winds or the frost,
  Or the whispering winds as they pass,
Or with all of lfe's ills to be troubled and crossed,
  Then to die as the withering grass.
Too pure was that heart and that life and that love,
Was the reason that she was transplanted above.

PARABLE OF THE PRODIGAL SON.—COMMENT.

THIS parable illustrates well
  Of father, son,—what tongue can tell,
  Parental love more pure;
For when the younger son became
Inspired throughout his youthful frame,
    His portion to secure,
Impatient waiting time (he thought) so long,
Asks for the portion which to him belong.

How true to nature was that child,
On thoughts of distant lands he smiled,
    Through visions of the far
And distant lands which overcome,
Which led him from his father's home
    To distant lands afar;
From that good father with paternal love,
An emblem of the one of all—above.

And though it grieved him to the heart,
His youngest son to with him part,
    Perhaps to ne'er him see;

His son so tender yet of years,
What sorrow and what silent tears
  Stole down his cheeks; so free,
To part with him who was his joy and pride,
And lost to him upon this world so wide.

In silent and in troubled look,
The father now upon him took
  His living to divide
With him, who never was away
From home one night before to stay;
  Or from his father's side
Long journey in far distant lands to take,
While that paternal heart is like to break.

But for a foreign country still,
His portion now has got, and will
  Soon with the harlots spent,
Until a famine came, and then
Now money gone he felt as when
  He from his father went,
Till in the fields, with want and hungar pine,
And longing for the husks they fed their swine.

But says, I will arise and pray,
Unto my father thus wll say:
  Dear father, I have sined.
'Gainst heaven, and in thy sight no more,
I am unworthy to restore,
  Or with thee e'er be kind,
Me make as one of thy hired servants meek,
So I may homeward go thy favor seek.

I will arise, to my father go,
The first resolve but made, when lo!
  In that direction went.
The father sees him far away,
His long lost son, he hears him say;
No messenger he sent,

But ran to him in the distance wide,
No vengeance then, or e'en his son did chide.

But arms of mercy arond him threw,
His long lost son, he yet him knew.
Though changed to human sight,
With harlots, though in dens did file,
Is yet his son, yet all the while,
Yet never did him slight,
But ran to meet him with that joy divine,
He saw him coming,—far from feeding swine.

What language can in justice dwell,
When that paternal heart did swell
With joy, to meet his child.
And ran to meet him with what joy,
His long lost son, his youngest boy,
From paths and ways so wile.
" Bring forth the robe so new," he says, " Put on,
And shoes upon his feet "—his long lost son.

Once dead is yet alive and sound,
His long lost son, he has been found.
A ring put on his hand,
The fatted calf is ordered killed,
With joy that father's heart is filled,
There's music o'er the land,
And dancing in that home, what joy and pride,
His long lost son is home now to reside.

What glory to this world to know
This Father is of all below,
The same to all his sons
And daughters on this earth and ours,
Where monuments of kindred towers,
And kindred blood still runs;
From age to age his sons begot the same,
And all of us from that same Father came.

I will arise, was all was said,
And who alive to vice so wed
    Of all his children now
But can the word repeat anew
To that same Father which so flew,
    And all will still allow
That that same Father now which distance mar,
Still sees his long lost children coming far.

"I will arise," who cannot say,
Though portion spent and far away,
    Long lost to sin and shame,
And altered by the lapse of years,
By trouble, and through sorrow's tears,
    None but ourselves to blame,
But sinning against Heaven and in His sight,
Not worthy to be called his son by right.

"I will arise, though steeped in sin,
And long lost from my father's kin,
    And unto him will say:
'Against thee I have sinned in sight
Of Heaven, long been from paths of right,
    Unworthy for to pray.'"
Now that same Father, filled with love and zest,
Still runs to meet his children east or west.

And when to meet them, on them place
His arms, his children's lineage trace
    In them, though long been lost
In paths so low in every line,
With harlots and of feeding swine;
    No matter where been tossed,
That Father sees us come, good and wise,
If we but to ourselves will say, "Arise."

REFLECTIONS

ON A RETURN VISIT HOME AFTER A TWENTY YEARS ABSENCE IN
CALIFORNIA.

I am home on a visit to be,
  My relations and friends for to see.
    Since I've been them among
    O, the time has been long,
And I want now to see if they will
Have remembered and thought of me still,
    And warmly greet me
    Whenever they meet me,
For the time has been long I've been gone,
Now I'll see who will welcome me home.

Ah, when first I left home in the Fall,
My poor mother was dead, which was all;
    But I've been so long out
    On a gold hunting scout
In the land so far off in the West
That I now hear of some of the rest
    Of my kindred have died;
    Yes, how many have died?
For now both of my parents are dead,
And my wife and her parents have fled.

O, dear nature of all what a change,
And how can I ever arrange
    In my mind this is so,
    That my folks are laid low,
And can never more see them alive,
Or can evermore hope to derive
    The joy for to see them;
    O, no, I'll ne'er see them ;
They are gone to their last resting place,
And how can I their memory efface.

They have moved to a house covered o'er
With green grass and a cold iron door,
   Where the wintet's winds groan
   On the granate and stone,
By the cheeks of that arch-covered door,
As I've mentioned and said here before;
   With its floor damp and cold,
   But they cannot take cold,
Nor the harsh flowing winters in flight
E'er disturb them, or wake them by night.

What a tenement thus to behold,
And so many for Death to enfold
   In his chilly embrace,
   In this grass-covered place.
Since I left here has made them his prey;
No! nor would he as much as delay
   Till I'd see them again.
   I'll ne'er see them again,
But from sorrow and trouble they're free
If they ne'er can again look on me.

What a house for to welcome within,
And so cold from so many of kin
   As they lay side by side,
   Where there's none to deride
In their house covered over with clay.
And with no one to envy or say,
   That they covet their home.
   In their still quiet home,
Where so damp and so chilly its breath,
And so cold and so silent in death.

They are laid side by side, two and two
As they should, for they lived their life through
   Without going away
   From each other astray;
Through the term of their natural life,
They have lived it all through man and wife,

Until death came along.
Ah, cold death came along,
And them summoned to pay him his tithe,
As when ripe for his sickle and scythe.

And they did not refuse, but rejoiced
For to lay where disturbance and noise
   Is all hushed in repose,—
   Where the still sleep of those,
And where family discord ne'er comes
To disturb in their still quiet homes;
   Or where strife is ne'er heard,
   Not a word is e'er heard
For to wake or disturb them asleep,
Nor is ever with grief caused to weep.

Now their sleep is so quiet and still
In that spot by the side of the hill,
   Where no dreams to disturb,
   Or vile passions to curb,
Or original promptings to wrong
Can e'er trouble or come them among;
   For their fate's all the same,
   All returning the same;
Their deep sleep everlasting decreed,
And from all further trouble are freed.

What can man have so good as still rest?
Or can kings, queens or princes be blest,
   Or with anything more
   Than what they have in store,
As they lie side by side all at ease,
And with no one to trouble or please,
   In all changes the same?
   For all things are the same
To them now in all shapes and all form,
And they ne'er can be woke by the storm.

They have brought with them all they can bring,
And are equal to prince now or king,
   As they lie there in state,
   Nature to recreate,
And come back to their mother again;
For as no one on earth can refrain
   In her bosom to lay,
   In her bosom must lay,
Or before they can fairly reach home,
To the bosom of earth all must come.

What can years be to them now, alas!
Or the centuries' roll as they pass;
   While the earth rolls around,
   With her age never found,
Or how long she was made before they
Were called forth from the planet of clay
   By the laws of their parent,
   Their natural parent,
With her laws true to nature sublime,
Ne'er consulted or asked them their time?

But since Nature has now had her will
And no laws but her own to fulfill,
   Or her purpose to be,
   And with none to agree
With humanity just as she may,
And no one but herself to obey,
   But herself for to please,
   Nothing adverse to please,
But is sovereign, all things in all
Could not make a mistake in their call.

Or to call mortal creatures to care
From they know not themselves nor from where,
   From the time they came forth
   To inhabit this earth;
Generations through life as they pass,
'Then to all be cut down as the grass,

Decompose all alike,
All return alike
To the place they were taken to live,
And then all which they got had to give.

O, no, Nature could ne'er been engaged
In so trifling a way, or have waged
Such a war to destroy
Those to life she employ
And exterminate them when she please;
As the ax to the root of the trees,
Or what pleasure to sport,
With poor mortals to sport,
With death's agonies filling the air,
And a dying in grief and despair.

No; as Nature could ne'er been engaged,
No, however so much she's enraged,
With humanity crossed
As the ocean is tossed,
Or her wrongs being never so much,
As with life here us poor mortals touch
With existence and life,
And creation and life,
And at will cut us down in distress,
And as leaving mankind no redress.

Long before human form wore a robe,
Long before there was life on this globe,
All was still and at rest,
Then with peace all were blest,
All humanity then was at ease;
And to say now or think as we please,
For then all never sinned,
No, for none ever sinned,
In the thousands of years without form
All infallible was until born.

And what vengeance was there to repay,
To disturb the dead slum'bering clay?
 And poor mortals create,
 And with mankind his mate,
Which has been on earth's surface so long,
Here in millions in prolific throng,
 But have perished and gone,
 Grown, and perished, and gone,
And returned to that place all the same,
And from which all humanity came.

And nature would have stopped long ago
To create and recreate so,
 If no purpose or way,
 Or had aught to obey,
But give creatures a glimpse of the sun;
Then their sad journey over and run,
 And come back then again
 To their mother again;
She would natural offspring refrain,
And would sicken from labor and pain.

There must something more grand to perform
Than give birth unto poor human form,
 Then to call them away
 To their cold house of clay,
Then on earth in her bosom to sleep,
And with no one alive who can keep
 From returning decay;
 For all must decay
And become, in the great lapse of time,
A still atom of Nature's own clime.

But who is there, if they had their will,
Just in peace would as leave have lain still?
 Here attached in some way
 To this planet of clay;
But in some way, we cannot tell how,
Yet as all will now think and avow

That in peace they have lain,
Yes, through centuries lain
In repose through those thousands of years,
And ne'er dreading the future with fears.

No, they never had a fear or a dread,
Or had read about what has been said
    Of a world to come,
    Or the teachings of some
That they came here without their consent,
And that all must alike be content
    With a lingering death;
    Though life struggling with death,
That another of terror awaits   .
From what Nature herself recreates.

No, who would not much rather have been void
And slept on a in peaceful alloid,
    To this planet secured?
    There was nothing endured,
Than to run such sad chances as these,
But to think of would chill and would freeze
    The blood of a tyrant,
    No monster or tyrant,
Or that anything ever was made
On himself would draw such a tirade.

And this world would have never been made
To revolve in the sun and the shade.
    If that was intended
    It soon would have ended,
Or would ne'er been a planet at all
To revolve on its axis as a ball
    In its sphere round the sun,
    In its course round the sun;   ·
No, it ne'er would been placed here so grand,
Or if nothing was better for man.

For this beautiful world so immense,
So that man cannot make much pretense

For to know or to be,
Or have time for to see,
Or sublimeness to near comprehend.
For the time is so short here we spend,
So uncertain and short,
Yes, uncertain and short,
Being so short and uncertain through life
By the ills prone to mortals so rife.

But the beautiful birds and their songs,
All so merry and joyful in throngs,
And ne'er thinking of death,
They inhale the sweet breath
Of the morning, the air then so pure,
And ne'er troubled, uncertain but sure
That no worse e'er awaits,
Fears a worse ever waits,
But the summers of life they enjoy,
And the sweet thrilling notes they employ.

And the beasts in the forest and tree,
Still so cheerful and playful ne'er see
In the future those ills,
Or a death-bed, which fills
Up the mind of poor man with such dread;
Or, that after or when he is dead
Still another awaits,—
In such fear still awaits.
In his mind still depicted is cast,
In his being, so long as it last.

And of all things in life here at large,
Was mankind here as lord, in his charge,
Yet the future he draws
For himself by the laws,
Which no reason can e'er comprehend,
Or the laws of Creation amend;
But for mankind alone,—
Yes, that mankind alone,—
Him, for which this great planet was made,
On himself should make such a tirade.

If the mind of mankind is above
All the rest, with life's gift as they move
    On this surface of ground,
    Where all life's to be found
In this beautiful world with its hills,
And it valleys, and forests, and rills,
    With the bloom of the flower,
    'Midst the grass and the flower,
All for man for to here contemplate,
And to never himself underrate.

If the lillies and blades here are clothed,
Why should man e'er become so much lothed
    With himself, or to think
    That the glorious link,
Or the pride of creation forgot,
Or that e'er was conceived such a plot,
    For to make him be less,
    Yes, to make him much less,
When so much he is better than they,
And which Scripture and Nature both say ?

They are now quite as rich as a king,
And their promise as good for to bring
    With them now to the tomb,
    Where for all so much gloom;
Where the rich and the poor are the same,
As for all in this poor mortal frame,
      For death is not partial;
    No death is not partial,
For the level he holds in his hand,
Levels rich with the poor of the land.

And although they were aged and frail
Yet relentless death did them assail,
    Nor ne'er thought of their age,
    Or did ever assuage,
Or let up till the last breath was drawn,
And then had them put under this lawn;

For death is cold-hearted,
  Yes, very cold-hearted.
Them he laid in this house covered o'er
With green grass and the cold iron door.

Now the grass which grows over their grave,
Or their tomb, or this house as it wave
    With the wind as it pass,
    But soon wither, alas !
And came back to the place it came forth;
So is all human kind from their birth,
    Grows, and perish, and falls,
    Yes, dies, withers and falls,
Follow after each other in mass,
As the withering, perishing grass.

But the spot is a beautiful place
For repose of humanity's race;
    Nature has made it so,
    And they rest well below,
'Neath its grass-covered roof in the shade.
    For as Nature has kindly thus made
    It so pleasing all round,
    Sloping gently all round,
From the top to the bottom so fond,
To this spot by the side of the pond.

And as Nature was good and so kind
As to shelter this spot from the wind,
    For in wintry form
    Is the snow and the storm,
But no cold do they feel as asleep,
Or the wintry storm as it sweep
    O'er this cold mound of clay,
    O'er this grass-covered clay,
With its cheeks of the cold granite stone,
As it stands by the pond all alone.

Round this circling pond there's a fence
Near the spot of so little pretense,

With some trees leaning o'er,
  As with grief they have bore;
Or in sorrow for those they have seen,
Or so many put under the green
   In this circular spot,
   'Neath this circular spot,
Where in Chelsea it's found to the east—
Is not large, but the greatest's the least.

Now sleep on, as you've all found your last
Resting place from the storm and the blast;
   May you all rest in peace,
   'Neath the grass-covered place,
Naught disturb you till God, when He will,
Calls his promise with all to fulfill,
   Or when Gabriel's notes,
   Calls to all with those notes,
Come to life or the dead to arise,
For as that is His purpose all wise.

THE RAVEN.

BY E. A. POE.

Once upon a midnight dreary,
While I pondered, weak and weary,
Over many a quaint and curious
   Volume of forgotten lore—
While I nodded, nearly napping,
Suddenly there came a tapping
As of some one gently rapping,
   Rapping at my chamber door.
"'Tis some visitor," I muttered,
  "Rapping at my chamber door—
   Only this and nothing more."

Ah! distinctly I remember,
It was in the bleak December,
And each separate dying ember
    Wrought its ghost upon the floor:
Eagerly I wished the morrow;
Vainly I had tried to borrow
From my books surcease of sorrow—
    Sorrow for the lost Lenore—
For that rare and radiant maiden
    Whom the angels name Lenore—
    Nameless here forevermore.

And the silken, sad, uncertain
Rustling of each purple curtain
Thrilled me, filled me with fantastic
    Terrors never felt before;
So that now to still the beating
Of my heart, I stood repeating,
" 'Tis some visitor entreating
    Entrance at my chamber door—
Some late visitor entreating
    Entrance at my chamber door;
    This it is, and nothing more."

Presently my soul grew stronger:
Hesitating then no longer,
"Sir," said I, "or madam, truly
    Your forgiveness I implore:
But the fact is, I was napping,
And so gently you came rapping,
And so faintly you came tapping;
    Tapping at my chamber door,
That I scarce was sure I heard you."
    Here I opened wide the door:
    Darkness there, and nothing more.

Deep into that darkness peering,
Long I stood there, wondering, fearing,
Doubting, dreaming dreams no mortal
    Ever dared to dream before;

But the silence was unbroken,
And the stillness gave no token,
And the only word there spoken
   Was the whispered word "Lenore!"
This I whispered, and an echo
   Murmured back the word "Lenore!"
   Merely this, and nothing more.

Back into the chamber turning,
All my soul within me burning,
Soon again I heard a tapping
   Something louder than before.
"Surely," said I, "surely that is
Something at my window lattice;
Let me see now what thereat is,
   And this mystery explore—
Let my heart be still a moment,
   And this mystery explore;
   'Tis the wind, and nothing more.

Open here I flung the shutter,
When, with many a flirt and flutter,
In there stepped a stately raven
   Of the saintly days of yore.
Not the least obeisance made he,
Not a moment stopped or staid he,
But with mein of lord or lady,
   Perched above my chamber door.
Perched upon a bust of Pallas,
   Just above my chamber door,—
   Perched and sat, and nothing more.

Then this ebony bird beguiling
My sad fancy into smiling,
By the grave and stern decorum
   Of the countenance it wore.
"Though thy crest be shorn and shaven,
Thou," I said, "art sure no craven.
Ghostly, grim and ancient raven,

Wandering from the nightly shore,"
Tell me what thy lordly name is
   On the night's plutonian shore ?"
   Quoth the raven: "Nevermore."

Much I marveled, this ungainly
Fowl to hear discourse so plainly,
Though its answer little meaning,
   Little relevancy bore;
For we cannot help agreeing
That no living human being
Ever yet was blessed with seeing
   Bird above his chamber door,—
Bird or beast upon the sculptured
   Bust above his chamber door,—
   With such name as "Nevermore."

But the raven, sitting lonely
On that placid bust, spoke only
That one word, as if his soul in
   That one word he did outpour.
Nothing further then he uttered;
Not one feather then he fluttered—
Till I scarcely more than muttered,
   "Other friends have flown before;
On the morrow he will leave me
   As my hopes have flown before."
   Then the bird said, "Nevermore."

Startled at the stillness broken
By reply, so aptly spoken,
"Doubtless," said I, "what it uttered
   Is its only stock and store,
Caught from some unhappy master,
Whom unmerciful disaster
Followed fast and followed faster,
   Till his songs one burden bore;
Till the dirges of his hope
   That melancholly burden bore
   Of 'never—nevermore.'"

But the raven still beguiling
All my sad soul into smiling,
Straight I wheeled a cushioned seat in
    Front of bird, and bust, and door;
Then upon the velvet sinking
I betook myself to linking
Fancy unto fancy, thinking
    What this ominous bird of yore,—
What this grim, ungainly, ghastly,
    Gaunt and ominous bird of yore
    Meant in croaking, " Nevermore."

This I sat engaged in guessing,
But no syllable expressing
To the fowl, whose fiery eyes now
    Burned into my bosom's core;
This and more I sat divining,
With my head at ease reclining
On the cushion's velvet lining
    That the lamplight gloated o'er,
But whose velvet, violet lining
    With the lamplight gloating o'er,
    She shall press, ah! nevermore.

Then, methought, the air grew denser,
Perfumed from an unseen censer
Swung by seraphim whose footfalls
    Tinkled on the tufted floor.
"Wretch!" I cried, "thy God hath lent thee—
By these angels he hath sent thee
Respite—respite and nepenthe
    From thy memories of Lenore !
Quaff, O, quaff this kind nepenthe,
    And forget this lost Lenore!"
    Quoth the raven, "Nevermore."

"Prophet!" said I, "thing of evil!—
Prophet still, if bird or devil!—

Whether tempter sent, or whether
  Tempest tossed thee here ashore,
Desolate, yet all undaunted,   •
On this desert land enchanted—
On this home by horror haunted—
  Tell me truly, I implore—
Is there—is there balm in Gilead?—
  Tell me, tell me, I implore!"
  Quoth the raven, " Nevermore."

"Prophet!" said I, "thing of evil!—
Prophet still, if bird or devil—
By that heaven that bends above us—
  By that God we both adore—
Tell this soul, with sorrow laden,
If, within the distant Aidenn,
It shall clasp a sainted maiden
  Whom the angels name Lenore—
Clasp a rare and radiant maiden
  Whom the angels name Lenore."
  Quoth the raven, " Nevermore."

"Be that word our sign of parting,
  Bird or fiend!" I said, upstarting—
"Get thee back into the tempest,
  And the night's Plutonian shore!
Leave no black plume as a token
Of that lie thy soul hath spoken!
Leave my loneliness unbroken!—
. Quit the bust above my door!
Take thy beak from out my heart,
  And take thy form from off my door!"
  Quoth the raven, " Nevermore."

But the raven, never flitting,
Still is sitting, still is sitting
On the pallid bust of Pallas
  Just above my chamber door;
And his eyes have all the seeming

Of a demon's that is dreaming,
And the lamplight o'er him streaming
  Throws his shadow on the floor;
And my soul from out that shadow
  That lies floating on the floor
  Shall be lifted—nevermore!

INDEX.